THE LION OF JUDAH

By Janice L. Dennie

Sign up for Janice's new release newsletter on her website: JaniceDennie.com
Facebook: janicedennieauthor
Twitter: jdennieauthor

KENTE ROMANCE
An Imprint of Kente Publications
P.O. Box 184
Jackson, CA 95642

ISBN-10: 096433496
ISBN-13: 9780964334977

Other books by Janice L. Dennie

Lion of Judah Series

The Lion of Judah (Aug. 2015)
Moon Goddess Queen of Sheba (Feb. 2016)
Menelik and the Lost Ark (Dec. 2016)

The Underwood's of Napa Valley Series

Kenton's Vintage Affair (Oct. 2014)
Justin's Body of Work (May 2015)
Carter's Heart Condition (Dec. 2015)
Brandon's Artistic Passion (Jun. 2016)

Dear Reader:

I wrote this book after reading an article that referred to the late Emperor Haile Selassie of Ethiopia as The Lion of Judah. After researching the topic, I learned that he and his family are descendants of King Solomon and the Queen of Sheba. This story is a work of fiction that stems from the powerful Lion of Judah dynasty that presided over Ethiopia for three thousand years, and the bloodline that flows through the title character, Prince Johannes. This edition reflects discoveries in information from when I wrote the book until now.

Prince Johannes of Ethiopia is torn apart by the escalating civil war in his country. Knowing a new constitution will end the war, he comes to the United States to finish the precious document. He never expects, however, to meet the woman of his dreams, especially when a deadly accident throws her literally at his feet. Shana Zachary has given up on relationships in general, men in specific, and doesn't intend to change her mind...until danger and intrigue force her to choose love.

Sit back, relax and enjoy reading The Lion of Judah!

Janice

Chapter 1

Prince Johannes pressed his back against the chapel door for cover, ducking a bullet flying over his head. The bullet struck a column, scattering chips of marble everywhere. He dropped to the ground and crawled to safety behind the church. As he lay on the ground, his shoulder throbbed from a recent bullet wound. Military training taught him to ignore pain. Royal training taught him not to let it show. Taking in deep breaths to regain his composure, he set his face into a nonchalant expression and slipped into the garage, walking at an even pace past his father's driver. Brushing the dust off of his unbuttoned shirt, he entered his family's estate through the garage door. A small gold lion crest bounced off his muscular chest as he climbed the elegant staircase.

Johannes stopped by to check on his father as he did every morning. His father had recently suffered a massive stroke that had paralyzed his entire left side. He knocked on the door.

"Come in, my son." Prince Dula, smiled when he saw his son enter the room. Though bedridden, Prince Dula retained most of his faculties except his slurred speech. Taking in a deep breath, he asked, "How does your shoulder feel?"

"I am fine, Father." Johannes pulled his customary chair to the side of the bed. Yanking a tissue from a box, he stopped the drool at the corner of his father's mouth.

"Son, promise me," he sucked in a breath. "You will leave the country—and finish those amendments." He thought about his son's latest bout with violence. "Without you—nothing else matters."

Johannes didn't want his father to over exert himself or worry. The long silence set him on the edge of his chair.

Prince Dula's right eye narrowed. "What if you had died in that assassination attempt?"

"I want to finish the amendments as much as you father," Johannes stated re-buttoning his shirt. Living through today's assassination attempt meant giving eighty different ethnic groups equal rights and protection under the constitution. But Johannes' adversaries would do anything to stop him from amending the constitution. Nevertheless, he had to find a way to get ahead of the assassins to save the future for his countrymen.

"You must achieve where I've failed, son. It is our last hope for peace."

Weary and frustrated from dodging bullets and looking over his shoulder, Johannes admitted the repeated attempts on his life prevented him from obtaining his goal. He had to finish those amendments because the fighting was turning into an outright civil war. As Johannes listened to his father rant and rave, his mind wandered off to the day they went to the top of a mountain. His father told him about their ancient ancestor Menelik I, a warrior prince who stopped the fighting among the surrounding tribes, forcing them to live in peace and submit to his leadership. The day his father told him the story, Johannes made a vow to pattern himself after Menelik I, and once again unite Ethiopia into a peaceful country. He planned to do it with the tip of a pen, not the barrel of a gun.

"And why can't you find a wife! You will be twenty-seven on your next birthday," his father said before coughing, snapping Johannes out of his daydream. "Do you hear me, son, are you listening?"

"Yes, Father, I am listening to you."

Every day, the same conversation—Johannes had it memorized. His father had become obsessed with finding a wife for him. As a boy, Johannes fell in love with a girl, but his father forbade the relationship because of her lack of royal blood. In the long years since, Johannes had affairs with different women from, Sweden, France, London, and the Caribbean, but he never gave his heart to any of them.

Harvard Law School had slightly changed Johannes—particularly two African-American women, both brilliant Rhodes Scholars. It was their intellect and sassy, urban attitude he found fascinating. He had never known women quite like them before. After meeting them, he hoped to find one like them, hopefully, a tall one, with long, sexy legs. But his father would never accept a woman who lacked a royal bloodline. His father was from a different generation. He held traditional ideas while Johannes, brimming with fresh, new ideas, dreamed of opening his country to auto manufacturing.

"My son, promise me you will leave soon."

"Yes, Father, I promise." Johannes kissed his father on his forehead and left the room to get on with his day's agenda.

As a member of Ethiopia's Orthodox Christian Church, every morning Johannes prayed for his country in his family's chapel. He had no idea an assassin's bullet lay in wait for him this morning at the chapel. After his morning meal in the dining room, he walked down the corridor leading to his office where he drank a demitasse espresso and read the Addis Daily News, Hadas Eritrea, and the Washington Post.

Very rarely did Johannes work outside of his family's massive mansion. The royals had left the national palace after the monarchy was abolished and replaced with a parliamentary government. The palace was now a museum.

Most of the time, ministers of the government

came by Johannes' family's residence to discuss bills passed in parliament, and political or church appointments.

As a modern-day prince, Johannes exercised his authority within the confines of the constitution. His goal was to secure the unity, sovereignty, and sanctity of Ethiopia by amending the constitution to promote peace and stop the fighting.

Rebecca, his pretty, middle-aged secretary, greeted him as he entered his office. "Prince Johannes, you have a visitor waiting for you in your office."

Bari Legesse, Johannes' childhood friend, sat in an armchair upholstered in a light-blue floral tapestry. His small frame stood at five foot five, which gave people the false impression he was weak, but he was not.

"Bari, my friend, how are you today?" Johannes said upon entering his office, which was heavily lined with legal volumes.

Bari very rarely came by unannounced unless he had a good reason. Johannes took one look at Bari's face and knew something was wrong. He wondered what bad news Bari brought. But whether the news was bad or good, one thing Johannes could say about his loyal friend was that Bari always spoke the truth. Bari stood up from his chair to shake hands with his lord and friend. Instead of taking Bari's hand, Johannes embraced him.

"I'm feeling well. How's your shoulder?" Bari remembered when it first became injured.

"I am fine." Johannes lifted his shoulder to show Bari he was in no pain. He walked to his desk and sat down.

Bari crossed his short legs and leaned back in the chair, both hands gripping the edge of the chair tightly.

"There was a riot yesterday near the Somalian border. A group of protestors applied for jobs at the Ethiopian National Bank. They were denied, and told the jobs were not open to them. Last week, violence occurred when a water main broke in a small town in the south. Government officials took their time coming. All over the country people are in revolt, Johannes. As you said, people are tired of being treated like second-class citizens."

"I read about both incidents from my daily dossier." Johannes' jaw twitched listening to Bari's account.

"Was anyone hurt in the riot?"

"No."

A champion of the underdog, Johannes' driving inner force to protect his countrymen ate at him. What angered him the most was that his countrymen consisted of indigenous people who looked similar but belonged to different ethnicities, all speaking different dialects. Would he ever be able to unify all of them?

"Yes, I know, Bari. I told you I'm going to end this fighting with the tip of a pen, not the barrel of a gun. I am leaving to finish the amendments," Johannes stated behind steepled fingers. He leaned back in his leather chair. "It is taking longer than I thought, Bari. My father thinks I will complete them faster outside the country."

"He's right," Bari asserted, uncrossing his legs. "I have wanted to discuss the amendments with you for a long time."

"I can finish them faster without the distractions here at home." It was obvious Johannes' enemies didn't want him to finish those amendments. He massaged his left shoulder where the gunshot wound still ached, unaware Bari casually observed.

Bari stood up and put his hands in his pockets and began pacing the room. He stopped and turned around. "While you're away, we will have more uprisings and revolts. What will we do to quench the violence?"

"I will take key representatives with me. We will meet on a daily basis. Together, we should be able to finish the constitution within a reasonable amount of time. General Motabe will handle any civil uprisings, and the Council of Representatives will continue to handle any administrative matters."

"Will you go to Uganda, Kenya, or London?" The tension lifted from Bari's face.

"I think I will visit Sifani in California." Johannes stood up and joined Bari at the large window overlooking the garden.

A smile crossed Bari's face. "I haven't seen Sifani in years. All three of us were like brothers when we were boys. Tell him I said hello." Then the smile faded from Bari's face. "I will miss you, Johannes. I will keep an eye on your father and sisters and call you every day."

Johannes looked into Bari's eyes and gripped his arm. "Thank you, my friend."

"When do you plan to leave?" Bari kept a tight hold on his emotions.

Johannes walked back toward his desk and looked at his calendar. "There is no sense in waiting. I will make plans to leave next week."

Chapter 2

Loose tendrils of long brown curls blew into Shana Zachary's copper face as she traveled south on the Golden Gate Bridge into San Francisco, humming to the music on the hip hop radio station. The twenty-five-year-old financial manager's Versace scarf whipped in the early August wind as she lowered the windows of her Tesla S convertible. She arrived in downtown San Francisco at approximately seven forty-five, as she did most mornings, and drove into the Transamerica Pyramid garage.

She slid her long, shapely legs out of the white leather seat and moved with smooth elegance to the elevator, exiting on the twenty-eighth floor. She pushed her way through a set of plate-glass double doors with the seal of the U.S. Foreign Aid Commission painted on with gold leaf.

Shana walked through a labyrinth of portable modular furniture leading to her private corner office. The striking view of the Golden Gate Bridge surrounded by harmonious mountains greeted her, as it had every day for the past three years.

She spoke French, Spanish, and Swahili fluently, and often relied on her language skills when negotiating her loans. She recently negotiated a loan agreement with the Mexican government and impressed Señor Latorre, the Mexican Minister of Finance, by conducting the entire process in Spanish.

Shana laid her briefcase on her desk, turned on her laptop, and dropped a pod of French Roast coffee into the brewer. After removing her filled mug, she leaned her five-foot-nine frame back in her leather executive chair and clicked on the icon for the Wall Street Journal. Every morning, before anything else, Shana read the WSJ financial page while drinking her coffee.

MEXICAN GOVERNMENT STRIKES OIL WITH U.S. GOVERNMENT LOAN! "Oh my God," Shana gasped to herself, almost spilling her coffee. "It worked!" she said out loud. She felt as though she had hit the lottery. It was a gamble she took when she included as one of the conditions of the loan that the Mexican government invest at least half of the U.S. funds in oil refinery equipment.

She quickly called Harry Withers, the Regional Administrator, and told him about the article. Minutes later, she heard his footsteps walking down the hall to her office.

"Well, where is the article, Ms. Zachary?" he asked. "I can't believe it. Numerous countries have been defaulting on U.S. loans." He read the article while looking over her shoulder. "I can feel a promotion in this for you," he said, licking his full lips. "The government will get its money back plus interest with this news."

"I followed up with Señor Latorre at Banco de Mexico two weeks ago," Shana said, looking up at him. "Remember, I told you I granted them the loan with a stipulation that half the funds go toward purchasing refinery equipment and developing oil fields in Central Mexico."

"Well, maybe you have intuition or something, but I know one thing, I'm going to get some positive feedback from Washington about this. I can almost guarantee we will both get promotions due to your good work on this project. Well done, Ms. Zachary. Job well done. Why don't you take the day off? You've been working lots of overtime."

As soon as he left, Shana got on the phone and called Lauren, her closest friend since childhood. Lauren's facial complexion was pale compared to Shana's, and her rail-thin physique lacked Shana's curves. Lauren picked up the phone after two rings.

"Hello?"

"Lauren, guess what?" Shana said excitedly.

"What?" Lauren replied dully.

"I'm taking the rest of the day off," she laughed. "Do you have plans for lunch?" She paused because it was early in the morning. "My treat."

"Your treat?" Lauren all of a sudden perked up. "I guess we can go out to lunch. What's the occasion?"

"Remember when I told you I would treat you to lunch at the Top of the Mark if I got a big promotion?"

"You didn't get it, did you?" Lauren asked in a loud voice.

"It's in the bag!" Shana replied. She could feel herself smiling from ear to ear.

"Well, good for you," Lauren said. "I always knew you'd get it one day. I've watched you work nights and weekends for years."

"Can you get off for a long lunch today?" Shana asked, clearing her desk.

"Can I . . ." Lauren paused. "Of course I can! I'll ask for some emergency leave. We shouldn't be gone for more than two or three hours, should we?" Lauren asked.

***

Shana and Lauren walked up the asymmetrical staircase leading to the restaurant. A young hostess led them to seats near the window. Minutes later, a handsome waiter with an Italian accent came over and took their order. Shana ordered sautéed salmon, pasta salad, and champagne. When the champagne arrived and was poured by the waiter for them, Shana raised her glass to Lauren. "This is my treat to you, Lauren. You are my best friend. I've known you since elementary school, and I want to share my happiness with you."

Lauren responded with a toast. "Shana, you know I've always believed you could accomplish any goal you set. You are like a sister to me. I am truly happy for you and your well-deserved promotion. Congratulations."

"A toast to us both!" Shana replied.

"So what do you have planned for this weekend?" Lauren asked.

"Oh, I may go to see Antoine Fuqua's new action movie Friday night. Want to go?"

"Sure!" Lauren replied.

"By the way, I knew I was supposed to ask you about something. How did your date go with Jason last weekend?" Lauren asked.

"He took me to an expensive French restaurant here in town."

"Oh." Lauren paused. "Which one?"

"Atelier Crenn."

"Did you enjoy yourself?"

"Yes. It was great."

"How was Jason's conversation?"

"Boring."

"Boring!? I took an evening class with Jason, we were both on the same team. He is a remarkably intelligent person and a good conversationalist. He's anything but boring."

"I'm sorry, Lauren."

"Explain what you mean by boring."

Shana took a sip of her champagne. "He talked about computers the entire evening. I'm not interested in computers or him, Lauren."

Shana remembered how Jason's face looked when she rejected his offer for another date. She told him she wouldn't be able to see him anymore for a while because she needed to work late hours and weekends for the next two months. She used her job as a shield, giving this line to anyone who asked for a second date. She'd gone out with him to please Lauren.

This stunningly beautiful, independent, unmarried woman had never been in a serious romantic relationship with a man. She never initiated or encouraged dating, but instead spent her time developing her successful career.

The death of Shana's parents had affected her deeply. She had no hope or intention of forming an intimate relationship with any man. She had told Lauren about her problem with intimacy many times. Lauren had advised her to seek professional help, which she did not do. Shana remembered Lauren telling her a special man would one day reach her heart. Until then, Lauren was going to introduce Shana to different young men, hoping that one day Shana would meet her prince.

Chapter 3

Johannes and his entourage of security officers, household staff, and key officials arrived at Kennedy Airport in New York City before dusk. Arriving at the airport reminded him of his first flight to the United States to attend Harvard University. He thought about his professors who affected his thinking, and the friends who opened his mind to American culture. He wished he had kept in closer contact with some of them. After refueling the chartered plane, the pilot continued the flight to San Francisco.

While en route, Johannes studied and memorized some maps of California to keep himself occupied. He fell asleep and dreamed of his childhood adventures with his friend Sifani.

When Johannes was a child, he longed for a brother, but his mother was unable to bear any more children after him. Sifani was the son of a chambermaid who lived in quarters on the family's country estate. Johannes' father forbade him to play with any children living on the estate. But being a friendly child, Johannes ignored his father and became Sifani's closest friend.

They found a hiding place in the ruins of a Christian church. Painted faces looked down at the two children from the limestone ceiling. Amidst the stares of those faces Johannes and Sifani spent the days of their childhood, playing soccer in the old courtyard and swimming in a creek.

Johannes treated Sifani like the brother he never had. He taught Sifani everything he knew. When he studied his homework, he studied with Sifani, and found that Sifani was gifted.

After leaving for Harvard, Johannes cashed in one of his trust accounts and secretly paid for Sifani's tuition to Stanford Medical School. Sifani eventually graduated and married a woman named Stephanie, also a medical student. They made their home in Palo Alto, California, near the medical center where they both worked.

Johannes dressed incognito while traveling. He wore blue jeans, a light-blue shirt, and casual loafers. No one would ever suspect his true identity. He'd asked his security guards to dress casually too, once they left New York.

He spotted Sifani and gave him enough hugs to last a lifetime. He looked at Sifani's wife with approval. He noticed they both wore their hair short and curly, and were of average height and weight.

Johannes walked with them down the escalator, his security following at a discreet distance. He told Sifani about the riots, fighting, and other violent activities going on back home.

“Where did you get your scar?” His eyebrows drew into a frown as he examined the scab above Johannes’ ear.

Johannes looked away. He didn’t want to talk about his recent attack.

“Please, Johannes, you must stay with me and Stephanie while you are here.”

Johannes declined. He had brought his chauffeur, Ali, and his head housekeeper, Ababa, to his family’s estate in Hillsborough, a neighboring city to Palo Alto. Tomorrow, he had plans to begin working on the amendments with his key representatives until it was finished.

“You must understand, my friend. I am not on vacation. My visit will be short. I am here to finish some amendments to our constitution, to unite our country and end the civil war. I will complete it faster if I stay at my family’s house in Hillsboro. I want no distractions, especially the kind friendship brings.”

“Forgive me, Johannes. Ending the fighting and completing the amendments are two monumental efforts. I want to do everything in my power to support you. Tell me what I can do to help.”

“Nothing. Be available for me in case I need you,” Johannes replied.

Sifani smiled. “You know I’ll be available for you.”

“Thanks.” Johannes looked at his friend and smiled. “I will spend one night with you and your wife,” Johannes offered with a wide grin.

When they arrived in Palo Alto, they all laughed, and the two young men reminisced about old times as young boys back home.

“So where are you working now, Sifani?” Johannes asked.

“Stephanie and I work out of Stanford Medical Center.” He was about to go into details when Stephanie interrupted him.

“He doesn’t want to hear about all of the boring details of your work.” She smiled at Johannes. “We should make plans to show him around the Bay Area.”

Sifani raised a skeptical brow at Stephanie and agreed she was right. “I know you did not come here to visit, but can you not take one day to spend with your old friend?”

“Okay. Okay. Why don’t we get together at the end of the week, on Friday? I’ll have some time off.”

"Where should we take him, Stef?"

"Let's take him to Sausalito," Stephanie said.

"Sounds good." Sifani looked at Johannes. "Do you want us to pick you up?"

"My chauffeur came with me. He studied all of the road maps for Northern California, and should know all of the roads by now. Besides, I went over several road maps myself during the flight. All I need is the address."

"Good." Sifani pulled a business card from his wallet. He wrote an address on the back of the card and leaned over to hand it to Johannes.

Johannes turned the card over. "Trieste Coffeehouse," he whispered under his breath. He turned it back over to the front and leaned back in his chair. "Doctor Sifani." The word Doctor touched his heart. "I am proud of you, Sifani," Johannes said.

"You made it all possible." Sifani looked Johannes directly in his eye. "So it is set. Your chauffeur will drive you to the address on the card this Friday. We'll meet you around seven o'clock. We can all have a bite to eat before going out for a night on the town. I promise I will show you a good time," Sifani said.

"I'll be at the coffeehouse," Johannes replied as he yawned and stretched his arms.

"Sifani, he's probably tired from the long trip."

"Why don't you spend the night?" Sifani offered.

"I think I'll take you up on your offer," Johannes said.

"I'll walk you to the guest room."

Johannes called his driver on his cell phone and told him to leave and come back in the morning. He stood up and walked with Sifani. Later in the evening, Johannes slept like a baby for the first time since the day he was shot.

***

The weekend came quickly. At precisely six forty-five, Johannes walked into the Trieste Coffeehouse. He'd arrived before Sifani and Stephanie. He was a stickler for being on time—another disciplined habit he picked up from his military training. The ambiance of the restaurant, with its nautical atmosphere, amused Johannes while he waited. He took a seat by a window overlooking the bay and asked the waitress to bring him a cappuccino and a copy of the local newspaper. He believed the best way to find out about a town was to read their local newspaper, which he did while he waited for Sifani and Stephanie.

Friday evenings were a special time for Shana—it was movie night. To keep up with the endless films coming out of Hollywood, she decided to reserve Friday nights for movie viewing, then she could spend the rest of the weekend working.

Tonight she decided to see the latest Antoine Fuqua action movie showing down the street from her townhouse. She checked the movie guide on her cell phone and saw that the next movie started at seven thirty. She looked up at the crystal clock on the mantle above the fireplace. It was six forty-five.

“Good, if I hurry, I can grab a cappuccino at the Trieste before the movie starts,” she said out loud.

The Trieste Coffeehouse was the neighborhood meeting place for local professionals, many of whom worked in San Francisco. It was located on a quaint tree-lined street laced with weathered storefront buildings, and literally sat on stilts over the water in the Sausalito marina. It was Shana’s favorite place to relax and have a cup of coffee or tea after a hectic day at work. It was also conveniently located down the hill and around the corner from her house.

Sapphire, her black-and-white tuxedo cat, brushed against her leg. “No, Saf, you can’t go outside, I’m getting ready to leave.” She pulled her rust-colored suede jacket from the hall closet and stuck her head outside to check the weather. Tiny beads of moisture formed on her face as she looked up at the overcast sky. The low-hanging clouds hung as silent as death. Something about the weather reminded her of a day she had longed to forget. She shook her head to clear her dark thoughts and whispered to herself, "No, I won't need an umbrella." She closed the door and locked it.

As Shana was heading down the hill, she sent a text message to Lauren. Lauren responded, "Shana, I'm sorry, I won't be able to make it to the movie with you tonight. Andre called and asked if I would go with him to Las Vegas this weekend. You know I'm not turning this getaway down. Hope you have fun, see you later."

Nearing the bottom of the hill, Shana smelled the aroma of freshly brewed coffee as she approached the Trieste Coffeehouse. "Ahh," she murmured. She could already feel the coffee warming her up this chilly night. She stood in front of the Spanish-style structure, admiring its clever display of maps and travel literature all arranged around the theme of coffee. She rubbed her gloved hand against the foggy window and saw the familiar rosewood board mounted on the wall listing imported coffees from Columbia to Tanzania in black calligraphy. A pretty waitress wearing a green apron over a white blouse greeted her when she walked in.

"I'll have a single mocha to go," Shana said as she took a seat at the counter. She looked around the coffeehouse and observed the empty tables.

Johannes happened to look up from his newspaper when Shana walked in. He quickly lowered the newspaper and tilted his head from behind the support beam partially hiding her from his view. He leaned back in his chair to get a better look at this stunning woman who commanded his undivided attention.

She moved with smooth elegance as she crossed the floor to admire the coffee flavors. Her long, curly, sable-brown hair was swept around her creamy neck, cascading loosely on her shoulders. Her eyes had a strange hazel-bronze tinge to them he found mesmerizing. Like fire, they flashed brilliant specks of bronze hues from her oval face. Her cheekbones were high and her lips soft and full. He could somehow sense the curvy silhouette of her body through her jacket.

Strong feelings of arousal took control of his consciousness as he leaned back in his chair, dazed by this vision of loveliness. He could feel his heart pounding. A quick flash of heat rushed through his entire body. His back became damp. Beads of sweat slid down the side of his forehead.

Johannes had his pick of women from all over the world, but he found something different about this woman. Never would he have thought fate would bring him across stormy seas and dry deserts to stand sweating like a scared schoolboy in front of this American beauty. *I can't let her get away*, he thought to himself. He needed to act before she was gone.

Shana walked to the counter and watched the waitress prepare her coffee in the sleek silver espresso machine. She casually glanced up at the nautical clock on the wall and saw that it was five minutes after seven. She nervously tapped the tips of her opal fingernails on the countertop.

"Can you put my coffee in a large cup?" She didn't want her coffee to spill as she carried it down the street.

Johannes stood up and walked toward the door.

The waitress saw Johannes staring at Shana from across the room and grinned. Shana turned around, prompted by the grin on the waitress's face. She met the smiling gaze of a handsome, clean-shaven, bronze-skinned stranger with broad shoulders and slim hips.

As he leaned against the doorway with his arms folded across his chest, Shana noticed he had a formal air about himself, almost regal, manifested by his perfect posture. She looked from his feet to the top of his head and thought she had never seen a man without a visible flaw. He smiled at Shana through dimpled cheeks. Shana raised one eyebrow, pursed her lips, and turned her back on him.

I'm not interested, she thought as she waited for her coffee.

"Two seventy-five." The waitress handed Shana her coffee.

Shana adjusted the lid on the coffee cup, picked up her receipt, and quickly peeled three dollars from a small wad of bills from her coat pocket and laid them on the counter.

On her way out, she whirled past the handsome stranger without making eye contact. Her money fell out of her pocket and flew in the wind behind her as she walked down the deserted street.

Johannes saw the bills flying in the air behind her. He quickly stepped through the door and caught the bills in both hands as they floated down to the ground.

As she made her way down the street, Shana felt badly about her rude behavior. She could have at least acknowledged the man, she thought. But today she didn't have time. She wanted to get to the movie theater.

Johannes quickly caught up with Shana and walked beside her.

"Excuse me, I saw you in the restaurant," Johannes said. He extended his hand to the woman. "You dropped this." He flashed his most beguiling smile as he handed her the money.

An electrical current moved from the tips of Shana's fingers to the top of her shoulder when Johannes touched her hand.

She slowed down to a gradual pace and raised one skeptical eyebrow. She slowly lowered it at the sight of his dimpled cheeks. Her father had dimples.

"Thank you," she replied. She detected a subtle accent when he spoke. Maybe he was from the Caribbean.

"It was nothing," Johannes said in a velvety voice. He searched her face for even a hint of acceptance, but instead was caught in the grip of her hazel-bronze eyes. They stared at each other for a moment that seemed like an eternity. She was even more beautiful up close, Johannes thought. His coal-black eyes gazed warmly at her beneath his thick brows.

"Allow me to introduce myself. I am Johannes Harar. A young woman should not walk alone at night. I would be happy to escort you to your destination," Johannes offered.

Shana decided not to encourage him by asking him questions. She could see the gentleness in his eyes and hear it in his voice. She eyed the black roman numerals on her watch and saw she had about twenty minutes left. "Thank you, but I'm on my way to the movie theater across the street. I don't want to be late."

Johannes frowned and stroked his chin. "By yourself?" he questioned. He couldn't understand why a gorgeous woman like her was going to the movies without a date. Millions of guys would take her to the movies—or anywhere she wanted to go.

"What's wrong with going to the movies alone?" Shana blinked her large, almond-shaped eyes, put a hand on her hip and wagged her head. "Has the thought ever occurred to you that some women might prefer to go to the movies alone?"

Observing her defensive attitude and her sassy facial gestures, Johannes took a step backward to reassess this challenging urban beauty. Her expressive eyes burned with defiance. Women never challenged Johannes. This was the first time in his life he'd interacted with a boldly assertive woman with a strong personality to match a man's. He loved it. He had a strange weakness for women like her, especially if they had long legs. He glanced down at her left hand and saw she wore no ring. He grinned.

"Look, thanks for walking with me. It was nice talking to you but I really must leave." She gave Johannes a quick smile and walked away with a quick pace. By the time she reached the end of the block, the streetlight had turned red. Johannes walked quickly to catch up with her and cried out "Please, wait!"

Standing at the red light arms akimbo, Shana turned her head around to face the handsome stranger. She continued walking while looking in his direction. She said in a calm, cool voice, "Look! I told you I don't want to miss my movie. Leave me alone!" She was getting irritated with this aggressive man. Though he was handsome, she silently wished she had never spoken to him. She stepped further into the crosswalk after the light turned green and said to the stranger, "I'm sorry, but I—"

While her words were still hanging in the air, a parked car partially hidden behind a tall evergreen tree unexpectedly pulled away from the curb, sideswiping her body onto the cold concrete curb and knocking her cell phone from her hand. Johannes' blood ran cold as he witnessed the accident in horror. The color drained from his face. For a brief moment in time, he didn't want to believe this was happening. He quickly ran to her side and bent over her unconscious body. He yelled at the driver, but the car continued down the road, unaware of the disaster it left behind. Johannes stood alone in the dark street wondering what to do with this unconscious beauty.

Chapter 4

Johannes picked up the woman's limp body and motioned for his chauffeur Ali, to help. Ali saw Johannes struggling with Shana in his arms. He pulled the limousine up to where Johannes stood and rushed out to open the back door. Johannes placed Shana softly on the back seat and entered on the other side.

"Where to Your Grace?" Ali asked.

I'll let you know in a moment." Johannes pulled out his cell phone and called Sifani who was on his way to the coffee house. He explained the entire incident.

Sifani pulled his car over and exited the freeway. "Call emergency 911," Sifani advised as he pulled into a parking lot.

"She's in my car right now," Johannes said in a controlled voice. He'd seen his comrades die in his arms in the military. He refused to let this woman die in his arms. "I insist on taking her to the nearest hospital right now!" Johannes said with a tone of authority.

"Take her to San Francisco General Hospital," Sifani said stroking his eyebrows. Knowing his place, he dared not defy a command given by

Johannes even though they were the best of friends. "They have an excellent Trauma Unit."

"Good. I'll meet you at the hospital," Johannes commanded, and then ended the call. "Ali, we're going to San Francisco General Hospital."

Ali turned on the limousine's GPS and drove above the speed limit to the hospital.

***

Johannes was admitting the woman in the Trauma Unit under the name of Jane Doe when he spotted John and Stephanie walking through the emergency entrance. He quickly met them at the door.

"Let me handle the doctors," Sifani said as he walked past Johannes. "Stephanie will stay with you until I get back," Sifani said walking through the double doors into the trauma unit. Johannes and Stephanie talked about the incident while they waited in the emergency room.

An hour later Sifani returned.

Standing, Johannes straightened his shoulders waiting for Sifani's diagnosis.

"She will be fine." Sifani's eyes were brilliant and intelligent.

Johannes exhaled. "Thank you my friend."

"She has no broken bones or internal injuries," Sifani said. "She is suffering from minor contusions to different parts of her body and a mild concussion. She will be awake within a couple of hours."

The two men stood face to face. "Where do you know her from?"

Johannes paced with stiff dignity. "We met over an hour ago at the coffeehouse."

"You should have called an ambulance to bring her here," Sifani warned.

Johannes abruptly turned around. "Why?" he asked waiting for an answer.

"You may not know this, but Americans are notorious for filing lawsuits."

"Lawsuits?" Johannes dismissed Sifani's statement. "She will not sue me," Johannes replied clutching his hands behind his back. "She'll probably be grateful I brought her here." He glanced at Stephanie.

Stephanie looked up at Johannes searching for a plausible explanation to back up her husband.

"I'm attracted to her Sifani." Johannes said looking at Sifani.

"You're attracted to her?" Sifani nearly collapsed into a chair as his knees buckled.

“Yes, I am,” Johannes glanced at Sifani sideways.

“I’ve never heard you talk like this before Johannes.” Loose folds of flesh formed on Sifani’s forehead as he listened to Johannes’ confession. He straightened up and cleared his voice. “What’s her name?”

“I don’t know. I was trying to find out when she was hit by a car.”

Sifani rubbed his aching forehead. “You’ve been in this country less than a week, and already you’re attracted to a woman.” He paused thinking about the ramifications of this catastrophe. He decided to leave it alone because when it came to matters of the heart, Johannes was a grown man.

Johannes walked Sifani and Stephanie to the emergency exit. “I am forever grateful to you for helping me with this situation. I knew I could count on you.” Johannes said resting his hand on Sifani’s shoulder.

“Aren’t you coming?”

“No. I can’t leave her alone. I’ll stay here until she wakes up.”

“Remember what I said about lawsuits.”

“Don’t listen to Sifani,” Stephanie said in a gentle voice. “My advice is to follow your heart.”

Johannes smiled as he watched them walk to their car. He waved at his security parked nearby in a black SUV, and one standing outside the door.

***

The next morning, Johannes asked a nurse about the woman's condition. The nurse told him; she was awake having breakfast.

"May I see her? Did you find out her name?"

"Are you a relative?"

"No. I brought her here."

"I'm sorry, but immediate relatives can see her before she is released."

"I'll wait for her out here. Would you let her know she has a visitor?"

"You bet."

Johannes had a million questions. He knew nothing about this woman, her name, where she lived, her family, nothing. During the car ride, he searched her coat pocket for some identification. He found the money he'd returned to her and a set of keys. No purse, wallet, driver's license or cell phone. She was admitted as Jane Doe.

Minutes later the nurse returned. "The patient will see you now."

The heavy metal doors squeaked as Johannes pushed his way through to enter into the recovery area. He walked into the woman's unit and stood above her with his hands clenched behind his back. He stared at her lovely face.

The woman looked up at him. "Who are you? How did I get here?" She asked in a raspy voice.

"My name is Johannes Harar. You were the victim of a hit-and-run accident. I brought you to this hospital."

"I remember you now," she gasped. "I saw you in the coffeehouse last night," she said going into a fit of dry coughs.

"You shouldn't try to talk too much. You're still recuperating. Why don't you take a sip of your water," Johannes said pointing to her cup.

"The nurse said I can leave this morning." She said between sips of water. "I have to go to work."

"Work! I don't think you're ready to go to work—not after being hit by a car last night."

"I'm sorry Mr. Harar. I forgot to thank you for bringing me here."

"Call me Johannes," he said smiling. "You're welcome. You never told me your name."

"My name is Shana Zachary."

“Shana Zachary,” Johannes whispered. “Do you have a relative I can call for you?”

“Thanks, but the nurse already offered to call my aunt.”

“Is your aunt going to take care of you?”

“No. She’s too old. I’m not going to bother her with this.”

“Who is going to help you?”

“Me.”

“You? You don’t have any friends or roommates who can help you?”

“I live alone.” Shana didn’t want to ruin Lauren’s weekend in Las Vegas.

Johannes took a step back. “Can you even walk?”

“I already tried to stand this morning. I’m a little wobbly, but I can walk.”

“Why don’t you let me help you, Miss Zachary? I have a large house with servants who can care for you until you are fully recuperated.”

“But, I don’t even know you.”

“The most important thing for you to know is you can trust me.” He held out the palms of his hands. “I want to help you.”

Shana thought about Lauren but changed her mind. “Why do you want to help me?” Shana wanted to find out his motives.

“Because you shouldn’t be alone at a time like this. I insist. Let me help you.”

“Thank you. I’ll stay at your house for a couple of days, but then I want to go home.”

***

The next morning, the sound of rattling dishes awakened Shana out of a deep sleep. She heard footsteps outside a large oak door to her room. She raised her head slightly and saw a short, stocky, gray-haired woman who looked to be in her late fifties enter the room carrying a silver tray.

“Good morning,” the woman said with a friendly smile. “What is your name?” The woman spoke with a heavy accent.

“My name is Shana.”

“Thana,” The woman pronounced incorrectly. “What a lovely name.”

She laid the tray down on the dresser and came around to the side of the bed and began fluffing Shana’s pillow.

“Here, see if you can sit up.”

“Thank you.” Shana felt comforted by the gentleness of the woman’s touch as she fluffed the pillow behind her neck.

“His Grace thought you might be able to eat something this morning,” the woman said, laying the tray on a night table next to Shana. She lifted a napkin revealing a plate of English scones and then poured Shana a cup of tea from the steaming hot teapot, handing the cup to her.

“See if you can drink this” The woman urged as she watched Shana patiently.

Shana winced when she tried sipping the hot tea.

“Are you okay?”

“Yes. I’m fine. Thank you.” Shana felt stiff. Even to lift the teacup left a soreness in her arm.

“Can I get anything else for you?” The woman began walking toward the door.

“Yes, I’d like to know your name.” It hurt Shana to move the muscles on her face, but she attempted a smile.

“My name is Ababa,” the woman said.

“A—ba,” Shana caught herself before she mispronounced her name. “You have been very kind to me. Thank you.”

The petite woman smiled and quietly left the room.

After drinking her tea and eating a scone, Shana moved the tray aside and spent the rest of the morning in a deep, peaceful sleep.

The next morning the sound of running water woke Shana up. She pulled herself up and tried to stand on the Persian rug. The throbbing pain in the back of her head seemed to lessen as time passed, but she felt her legs tingle when she tried to stand. The heady scent of orange blossoms along with the humidity of the running bath water drifted toward Shana, stimulating her weak body.

Ababa came from the bathroom when she heard Shana getting out of the bed. "I take it you are feeling better now. His Grace said you might be able to get around by now. I am very happy to see he was right. As you can see, I am in the midst of preparing your bath. Do you feel up to it?"

"Yes, I do. I feel much better."

Shana stopped a moment and thought about what Ababa said.

"His grace? Who are you referring to?"

"I am speaking of Prince Johannes, Miss," Ababa replied softly.

Raising her head slightly and out of curiosity,

Shana asked, “Why do you call him Prince Johannes?”

“Because of his royal bloodline.”

Shana gave Ababa a confused look. “Royal bloodline? Where is he from?”

“Ethiopia. He is a direct descendent of King Solomon and The Queen of Sheba.”

King Solomon and The Queen of Sheba, Shana mumbled to herself. “You mean like King Solomon in the Bible?”

“Yes, Miss.”

Shana was at a loss for words. She’d seen European royal families, such as Prince William, on the news all the time. But, she never gave royal families from Africa a second thought. “Wow,” she uttered to herself. “Do you need help getting into the tub?”

“I think I can manage Ababa. Thank you.”

Ababa pointed to what looked like a doorbell situated next to the light switch in the bathroom. She told Shana to ring it if she needed anything.

Shana walked further into the huge spa-like bathroom and saw a plush, salmon-colored bath towel draped over a marble Jacuzzi along with a tray of scented soaps and oils.

"I laid some clothes out for you in the next room," Ababa said before leaving. "I will be downstairs preparing a meal for you and His Grace. If you should need anything, press the button," Ababa stated.

"Thank you again, Ababa. You're very hospitable."

A bath was what Shana needed. It seemed as though every bone in her body was still sore from the accident. She held on tightly to the guardrails on the tub. She dipped her toe into the steaming hot water before sliding down. Immediately the warm water penetrated her dry, parched skin, transforming it into a silky texture. "Ahh," Shana murmured as she closed her eyes and lay back in total relaxation.

As she lay in the tub, horrible scenes of her accident flashed across her mind. She saw Johannes walking toward her in slow motion, then felt pain in her entire body, then nothing. Her eyes fluttered open at the sound of voices. She leaned over and looked through a set of plantation blinds above the Jacuzzi, but she couldn't see anyone. She squinted her eyes to see better and saw a man and a woman standing against a white Jaguar. The woman was shapely, well dressed and seemed to be upset, as she clutched the sleeves of the man's jacket, violently shaking him as she sobbed. Shana ignored the s

The warm temperature of the water and the heady scent of orange blossoms had a soothing effect on Shana, temporarily casting her once again into a deep sleep. She dreamed of being attacked in the dark. Suddenly a man came out of nowhere and saved her life. Thirty minutes had passed while Shana soaked in the tub. When she awoke, she stepped out, wrapped herself in the plush towel, and went into the next room.

She observed the ornate Baroque furnishings spread throughout the room. She looked further and saw a beautiful gown draped across the canopied queen-size bed Ababa had made up. She walked over to get a closer look and held up the gown against her body, admiring its splendid beauty through a full-length mirror. Bronze and gold embroidery embellished the hem, sleeve edges and the neckline embellishing the garment in a detailed geometric pattern resembling a mass of crosses. She admired matching slippers, with the same pattern of crosses, laying on the floor beneath the gown. Shana had never seen such exquisite embroidery before.

The sound of screeching tires startled Shana as she dressed. She couldn't stop thinking about this Prince Johannes. The thought occurred to her, he was the man with the woman in front of the Jaguar. When she finished dressing, she looked in the mirror and smiled. She didn't look half as bad as she thought she would. The colors in the gown amplified her hazel-bronze eyes. The low cut bodice revealed her full round breasts.

She walked over and opened a set of French doors to a small terrace overlooking a garden with a miniature waterfall pouring into a pond filled with pink lotus flowers. The sweet fragrance of the August summer breeze drifted through the long spiked leaves of the tall California palms flanking the terrace. She inhaled deeply and let the fresh air clear the cloudiness lingering in her mind.

Chapter 5

Johannes sat at the dining room table reading his tablet and drinking a demitasse espresso when he saw Shana descend the staircase. She was a vision of loveliness. He immediately arose, his eyes watching her every step as she slowly approached him. When he saw her wearing the native Ethiopian gown, he thought about his homeland. Her footsteps were graceful as she crossed the parquet floor to meet the handsome gentleman standing at the table.

Shana smiled as she looked around. She could not believe the lavishness of the surroundings; each object was more beautiful than the next.

"I see you are well enough to join me for breakfast today," Johannes stated with a thoughtful smile.

"I'm feeling much better today. I lost my cell phone in the accident. I hope you don't mind, I used your land-line upstairs to call my best friend, Lauren. She's going to pick me up this afternoon."

"It's nothing," Johannes said. "Are you sure you are well enough to travel?"

"I think so. I want to thank you and Ababa for your hospitality. I hope I haven't put either of you through too much trouble."

Johannes gestured for her to sit.

"In my country it is our custom to give strangers, especially beautiful ones, good hospitality." Johannes eyes sparkled as he scanned Shana's creamy breasts partially revealed through the low-cut bodice.

Her slender hands unconsciously pulled up the bodice to cover her cleavage, but the gown was too large and kept slipping down.

"Please, you must eat something now. I took the liberty of having Ababa prepare several dishes for you since I had no idea what you preferred for breakfast."

Shana could not believe her eyes. The ornate buffet table was filled with eggs prepared several different ways, assorted muffins, breads, croissants, meats, mounds of fresh fruit and various condiments. She placed a croissant and some eggs on a saucer and came back to her seat.

Johannes' mind focused on the mystery surrounding, Shana. He hadn't had a chance to talk to her in detail and knew very little about her. All he knew was she possessed an independent spirit and a sassy attitude he found alluring. Most of the women he knew had never challenged him the way she had in Sausalito. He had to get to know her better.

"Shana, tell me something about yourself." Johannes asked as he watched her nibble on a blueberry muffin. "Where do you live? Who are your parents? Please tell me more about yourself." His eyes glistened like glass as he spoke honestly. "I am very curious to know everything about you."

Shana was not prepared to answer all of his questions. She had no intention of telling him everything about herself. It took her a while to gather her thoughts. "Why don't you ask me one question at a time?"

Johannes felt slightly embarrassed. "Where are you from?"

"I was born in Chicago, but I raised in California."

"Who are your parents?"

Shana frowned. "My parents are dead." She gave him an honest look. "My mother's name was Catherine, and my father's name was Robert." Shana saw he had a sensitive look on his face.

"I'm sorry," he said in a soft voice.

Shana could feel old wounds opening up. Losing her parents in an accident was her reason for avoiding intimate relationships with men. It was her deep-seated secret she never discussed with anyone. It was her way of protecting her heart from pain and loss. She didn't want to talk about her parents, and it showed on her face.

"You don't have to talk about them if you don't want."

"Thank you," Shana said exhaling.

Johannes thought about how the death of Shana's parents must have affected her. He knew he would have to handle her gently. He decided not to ask her any more personal questions. He needed to give her some space and time to open up to him.

He reached over and poured hot tea into her cup. Ababa had told him she liked the beverage.

"Thank you." Shana smiled and took a sip of her tea. She didn't like revealing too much about herself, especially without receiving information in return.

"Johannes, do you mind if I ask you a question?"

He looked at her. "What do you want to know?"

"Is it true you are a descendant of King Solomon?"

Johannes looked up and laughed as he removed the cloth napkin from his lap, placing it on the table.

"I assume Ababa has been talking to you about me."

"Well, is it true?"

"Yes. It's true."

"Tell me about your family," Shana asked with an inquisitive look on her face.

"It is a long story. You would not be interested."

"No, no, please tell me."

Johannes looked at her, dreading the long story. He was more interested in hearing about her life than discussing his. But to please her, he began to tell her his family's story. "According to Ethiopian history, Menelik was the son of King Solomon and the Queen of Sheba. He founded Ethiopia in the tenth century B.C." Johannes glanced over at Shana and focused on her reaction. He saw she was captivated. Leaning back in his chair, he continued. "All who can lay claim to this lineage are considered to be part of our monarchy and given the title Prince or Princess."

"Like Prince William and Princess Kate," Shana whispered.

Johannes nodded his head. "Ours is similar. The difference is the British monarchy has not been abolished. Our monarchy has been abolished and no longer has absolute political power. We exercise our authority within the confines of our constitution.

Today, Ethiopia follows a parliamentary system of government. The prime minister is the actual head of the government."

Shana sat quietly thinking about the story and how it sounded like something out of a fairytale. "Why are you here in the United States?"

"I'm sorry, but I cannot answer your question. My reason for being here is of national security." Johannes' life was in danger. He had an army of private volunteer security along with the protection of some UN security forces because someone didn't want him to amend the constitution. He hoped he could present the amendments to Ethiopia's political powers for a vote before it was too late.

Shana stared at her cold tea. "National security," she echoed. *I guess we both have secrets*, she thought, thinking about her secret surrounding intimacy. What an interesting man, she thought. "This conversation has been great. I wish I could stay and hear more, but I need to get home and get ready for work. She started to rise, after tapping the corners of her mouth one last time with her cloth napkin.

Johannes grabbed her hand. "I'm happy you have recuperated, but I'm sad to see you leave. Please allow me to drive you home. Call your friend Lauren and let her know I'll take you home."

"Thank you, Johannes. Let me know how much money I owe you."

"Nonsense."

***

Ali opened the back door of the limousine for Shana and Johannes. On the way to Shana's house, Johannes felt nervous about asking Shana if he could see her again. Over and over he thought of what words to say. When the car stopped and parked in front of her townhouse, Johannes felt slightly nervous but came out with his question. "Shana, I am very much attracted to you. May I see you again?"

"Um…I…Uh." Shana fumbled for words. She was grateful for how Johannes patiently looked after her, nursing her back to health after her accident. She was truly intrigued by this man's unusual background. But she couldn't allow herself to get romantically involved with him or any other man.

Johannes nodded his head at Ali through the rear view mirror, before opening the back door of the limousine. He walked over to open the door for Shana and held out his arm to anchor her step.

When Shana took his hand, a warm sensation stirred in the pit of her stomach. She could have sworn a bolt of electricity ran up the length of her arm. Time seemed to stand still for a moment. She looked up at him through thick lashes. Her mouth couldn't find the words.

Johannes looked down at her and thought he would melt in the warmth of her hazel-bronze eyes. He slowly walked her to the front door holding her clothes in one arm and supporting her body with the other arm. Once they reached the door, he watched as Shana fumbled to open the door.

"Here, let me help you." Johannes laid Shana's clothing across a white wicker chair on the porch and turned the key in the door knob. After he'd opened the door, he placed the key into her palm not forgetting she still had not answered his question. He asked her again. "Shana, I am fond of you. Can I see you tomorrow?"

Unable to say no to this kind man, Shana reluctantly agreed.

Chapter 6

For the next week, Shana stayed at home to recuperate and regain her health. She called Mr. Withers and told him about her accident. He told not to worry about her workload, she could work from home until she fully recuperated. She made an appointment with her primary care doctor and found out she was fine. Her doctor encouraged her to take a month off from work. Shana ignored her doctor's advice. She hadn't broken any bones. Why should she stay at home? She made plans to return to work Monday morning.

Johannes called every day to check up on her. As the days passed into weeks, Shana began to look and feel like her old self again.

Shana called Lauren over for Saturday morning brunch. After Lauren arrived, Shana pulled out an aubergine upholstered chair from the glass dining room table while Shana poured champagne mimosas in two long-stemmed crystal flutes. They dined on fresh fruit compote, poached eggs and muffins. Lauren had her back to a picture window overlooking a private marina lined with schooners, sailboats, and yachts. Stirring artwork by Atlanta's hottest black artist hung on her dining room walls.

Shana stopped and drew in a deep breath. “I have something to tell you, Lauren.”

“What?”

“Remember I told you about meeting Johannes at the Trieste coffeehouse, and about getting sideswiped by a car, and recuperating at his estate. I didn’t tell you something else very interesting.”

“Tell me! Quit leading me on Girl.”

“I found out Johannes is a prince. He’s a descendant of King Solomon and Queen Sheba.”

Lauren gave Shana a blank stare. “What?”

“Wait a minute, I have something to show you.” Shana went into her bedroom and pulled out the gown and slippers she wore when Johannes brought her home. She draped them across Lauren’s lap.

“What are these?” Lauren asked with a curious look on her face.

“These are the clothes I wore home from his house. My new suede jacket is ruined.”

“No. Not your new suede jacket from Neiman Marcus?”

“Yes, my new suede jacket,” Shana mimicked.

Lauren remained quiet for a moment trying to process what her friend had told her. “You know

Shana I can't believe this story. Why did you wait to tell me about this?" Lauren asked. "This Prince Valiant guy sounds like a fairytale come true. But you know royals marry each other. Don't get your hopes up because he probably won't marry you."

"Who's talking about marriage? I think it's interesting to meet a prince."

"Well sometimes royals marry commoners," Lauren said rethinking her position. "You've got to keep a positive attitude," she said. "So, are you going to go out with him?" Lauren asked leaning back in her chair.

"Yes, I'll go out with him, but I don't want to lead him on because, like you said, royals marry each other. Even if he did want to marry me, what do I have in common with him? I wasn't raised to live like a princess."

"Do you think Michelle Obama had thoughts like that when she became first lady of the United States?"

"She's not royalty."

Lauren gave Shana a frustrated look. "She's married to the leader of the free world," she said emphasizing the words free world.

"I'll go out with him one time, but I definitely can't get serious about him."

"I can't get serious about him," Lauren mimicked. "I wish I had one-tenth of your looks Shana," Lauren said scanning her friend from head to toe.

Shana turned her head away to look at the boats sailing in the marina through her dining room window.

"Haven't you noticed every time you meet a nice guy, you always find something wrong with him," Lauren said as she followed Shana to the kitchen.

Shana led the way back to the dining room carrying a pot of hot tea. "Like I said, Johannes is a Royal Prince. What do I possibly have in common with him?"

"Well for starters, you're both human. You both bleed; you both feel pain; you both eat, drink and sleep. Shall I continue?"

"He probably comes on to every woman he meets. I have no romantic interest in the man." She handed a teacup to Lauren, offering her a phony smile.

Lauren looked into Shana's eyes while swirling milk into her tea.

Shana wouldn't admit it, but thoughts of Johannes had lingered on her mind all morning. She sat daydreaming for a moment as her lips softly brushed the rim of her teacup. She tried to convince herself, Johannes was a very important, attractive man with whom she had absolutely nothing in common.

"Um, Um, Um, you're pitiful, Girl," Lauren said. She finished her tea and walked into the living room. Standing in front of the sliding glass doors, she stared out into the marina. "Tell me more about this prince," she asked, examining her long red fingernails.

Shana sipped slowly from her teacup. "He's in his late twenties, and he is extremely handsome like I told you, plus he has the sexiest dimples I have ever seen." She looked at Lauren, who by this time had a dreamy look in her eye. "And guess what? He asked me to go out with him tomorrow night."

"Where are you going?" Lauren asked as Shana took their empty teacups to the kitchen.

"I have no idea. I have to admit, I'm curious."

Lauren picked up her coat to leave. "I can see you are attracted to the man, I think you should give him a chance. Let your guard down. You can't be waving off love all the time. I'll call you next week, and we'll get together for lunch and talk some more."

Shana closed the door behind Lauren and sank into her plush white sofa. She thought about what

Lauren had said. *Maybe I should give him a chance*, she thought.

Later in the evening Shana prepared a steaming hot bath, and soaked herself. Her mind drifted on and off to Johannes until it was time to get out. She slipped into a white silk teddy, set the alarm clock and slid into bed.

***

The sound of the alarm woke Shana as she became a slave to the routine she knew well. She walked briskly out of her townhouse at seven thirty wearing a navy blue tailored suit. She drove past the drug store, gas station and then crossed the Golden Gate Bridge. She arrived at work within the usual forty-minute commute.

When she walked into the office, she could see outlines of Sheila standing in Mr. Withers' office. His voice was loud and commanding.

"No, I haven't heard anything from her yet, Sheila. She told me she'd be in today. Call her at home again."

Shana overheard their conversation on the way to her office. "Don't bother to call my house Mr. Withers, I'm here."

Sheila walked passed Shana on her way out.

Mr. Wither's looked up and saw Shana standing at his door.

"You wanted to meet with me today at ten o'clock?"

"Oh yes. Ms. Zachary, I wanted to check with you to find out if you finished those final reports for Banco De Mexico."

"Yes, I finished them several weeks ago. I put them in Sheila's inbox." After telling him in detail about her accident, Shana left his office walking down the sun-drenched corridor to Sheila's office. She found her reports still sitting in Sheila's inbox. She picked them up and brought them back to Mr. Withers. She went into her office and called her aunt.

Helen Jemison was a tall woman with greyish-white hair, beautiful clear skin, and shiny ebony eyes. She had spent the early part of her adult life raising Shana. She avoided bringing men around Shana. She concentrated on being a good elementary school teacher. She never married or had children of her own. Now retired, she sat at the kitchen table with the newspaper spread out, shelling peas. She cooked every day for her neighbor, Mrs. Brown, an invalid and the senior center down the street. She had taken two pies out of the oven and set them on the rack to cool when her phone rang.

"Hi, Auntie Helen," Shana greeted.

“Shana Baby, how you doing.”

“I’m fine. I called to check up on you.”

“Oh, I’m fine baby.”

“How are you situated for money auntie? Did you get the check I sent you last month?”

“Yes, I did darlin. Thank you.”

“I don’t know why you keep sending me money. You know I never go anywhere to spend it.”

Shana made a mental note to send her aunt another check.

“Auntie, I have something to tell you.”

“What is it darlin’?”

“Auntie, I met a prince.”

“A what?”

“A prince, Auntie, a prince.”

“What kind of prince, baby?”

“He’s an African prince.”

“Oh. How interesting—what country?”

“He’s from Ethiopia. He is a descendant of

King Solomon, as in the Bible. Auntie, he wants to go out with me, and I don't know what to tell him."

"Well, do you like him, honey?"

"He's real nice."

"Well, if he's real nice, then you should go out with him darlin'. You don't want to end up like me, a lonely old woman. I once had a young man interested in me when I was your age. Come to think of it, I thought of him as a prince too. He was polite and kind to me and your mamma. But I never gave him a chance." She stared into space. "Baby, don't make the same mistake. I'd give anything if I could go back in time and marry Marcus. Remember this life is not a dress rehearsal."

Shana thought about what her aunt said. She wondered what her life would be like when she became an old woman. She knew one thing. She didn't want to be old and lonely.

"Okay Auntie, I'll take your advice into consideration. I love you."

"I love you too Baby. Goodbye."

Shana spent the remainder of the day catching up on her backlogged work. She couldn't stop thinking about Johannes and how she was going to handle this situation. On the one hand, she wanted to take her aunt's advice, but then on the other hand her gut cautioned her to tread slowly.

Five o'clock came quickly. Shana drove straight home through the heavy traffic with Johannes on her mind. She couldn't shake him off.

Once she arrived home, she kicked off her shoes, turned on her Bose station, and drew a bubble bath. A moment later the phone rang, and she knew who it was.

"Hello Shana. How are you feeling today?"

She hesitated, torn between conflicting emotions. "I'm feeling fine." Still unsure of how to handle Johannes, she heard little if any of his conversation. All she knew was she had to stop Johannes because he was getting too close. Death had snatched away those closest to her. She vividly remembered the tormenting nightmares she had of her parents' dead bodies floating across the waves, and then slowly sinking toward the ocean floor, where they remained forever in their watery graves. Her parents' accident had taught her at an early age never to get close.

"Are you there?" Johannes asked.

"Yes. I have a lot on my mind."

"Are we still on for tonight?"

"Um hum," she replied, thinking about how to tell him to stop pursuing her.

"Then I will pick you up at seven thirty."

"Okay Johannes, I'll see you then. Good-bye."

As Shana prepared for the evening, she chose to wear a bronze knit dress with matching suede sling backs. She swept her heavy waves behind her shoulders revealing chocolate diamond earrings. She fastened her matching bracelet when she heard the doorbell ring. She pulled out her coat from her closet and walked downstairs to meet Johannes.

When she opened the door, Johannes had a surprised look on his face. This was the first time he'd seen Shana dressed up since her accident. He was delightfully surprised to see, how stunning she looked wearing a dress showing off her long legs. He scanned her face and saw the dark bruises and scratches along her hairline and temple had vanished. The metallic colors of her dress brought out the fire in her hazel-bronze eyes. For a moment, he looked her over admiring her beauty, wondering if she knew the depths of his desire for her. He stepped closer, instinctively taking her hand into his. He raised it to his lips, and kissed it seductively. "Shana, you look beautiful." He took her by the arm, making his claim, and thought, tonight, I will let her know how I feel.

"Thank you for the compliment, Johannes." She promptly locked the front door and walked with Johannes toward the limousine. She smiled and greeted Ali standing by the open car door as she approached the long black vehicle.

Ali didn't return a smile or say a word but gave Shana a blood-curdling stare, which Johannes did not see. Ali took Highway 101 to Hillsboro, then exited the freeway to approach the mile-long private road leading to Johannes' twenty-six-room estate.

During the familiar ride, Shana felt uneasy. She couldn't concentrate on Johannes' conversation because she kept thinking about how to tell him she wasn't interested in pursuing a relationship. When they arrived, Ababa greeted them at the door and took Shana's coat. They both walked into the library. Shana sat down on the black leather sofa while Johannes walked behind the bar.

"Would you like a cocktail?"

"Sure, I'll have one."

Johannes prepared two extra dry martinis, then walked back toward the sofa.

"Let us make a toast to your health," Johannes remarked as he handed a full martini glass to Shana.

Shana raised her glass to meet his in the toast.

Johannes put his glass on the coffee table and sat down next to Shana.

"So tell me, Shana, what do you do with your leisure time?"

"To be honest with you, I don't have a lot of

leisure time. My job is demanding." All Shana could think about since returning to work was getting her big promotion. She inherited a strong work ethic from her parents who raised her to be an achiever.

"Oh, come on. You cannot possibly spend all of your time at work."

"Well let's see, hmm, I enjoy playing chess, listening to music, dancing, movies, and traveling."

"Where have you traveled to?"

"I've traveled to Africa, Europe, and South America, mostly on business. I recently traveled to Rome and Greece for pleasure."

"When did you go?"

"Last summer."

"Did you enjoy yourself?"

"Yes, I did. Walking through the ancient ruins was like walking through time. I've seen the ruins of the ancient Mayan empire in Mexico too. My next adventure is to travel to see the Egyptian pyramids and maybe take a cruise down the Nile."

Johannes raised his eyebrows, impressed with her global exposure.

"You said you enjoy dancing."

"Yes. I do," Shana replied. "I love ballet. My favorite dance company is the Dance Theatre of Harlem."

"Oh, really, what do you love about them?"

"Have you ever seen them dance? I'll guarantee you've never seen a dance company like them before."

"And chess, where did you learn to play chess?"

"My father taught me."

A smooth song echoed through the invisible speakers. Johannes took her drink from her hand and placed it on the baby piano.

"May I have this dance?" he asked as he pulled her up toward him. She was reluctant at first but decided to stand up and face him. She followed his slow movements to the soft filtered music. She fit like a glove in his strong, powerful arms wrapped around her. She could feel his muscles through his clothing with every movement he made. Her stomach fluttered as she deeply inhaled the sexy scent of his cologne. When he spoke her name, almost a murmur into her ear, her eyes closed momentarily.

The sound of his silky voice and the twirling from the dancing was beginning to make her feel dizzy. Johannes stopped motionless for a moment and tilted her chin with his index finger, drawing her face closer to his. He kissed her slowly and languidly exploring the recesses of her mouth. Somewhere buried deep within her soul, a small spark ignited and flashed through her entire body awaking sensual feelings. He moved his mouth over hers, devouring its softness. His drugging kisses sent spirals of ecstasy through her body leaving her mouth burning with fire. Raising his mouth from hers, he gazed into her eyes. "Shana, you have stolen my heart."

Shana hadn't heard a word he said, because she hadn't expected his kiss to feel good. Quickly regaining her composure, she pushed away from his embrace in an attempt to discourage him.

"Are you okay?"

"I'm fine Johannes. I have something to tell you."

"What is on your mind?"

Shana took a deep breath and braced herself. "I'm not sure how I feel about dating you. I don't want you to think I'm ungrateful because I do appreciate how you helped me and all, but I...."

Her deep-seated fear of intimacy lifted its ugly head, overruling her mind. On a deeper level, she was genuinely attracted to Johannes, but she'd convinced herself a relationship with him would never work because they both came from different cultures and backgrounds. She believed if she continued to date him, he would get hurt. She didn't want to hurt him because she liked him as a person. She didn't have the heart to encourage this kind man. She had to put an end to it.

Walking away from him, she said in a calm voice, "Johannes, I am fond of you, but I'm not interested in a romantic relationship at this time in my life. I think we should remain platonic friends. I'm sorry."

Johannes hid his astonishment well, but he was devastated. His voice dropped. "No dinner tonight?"

She shook her head. "I'm not hungry." She'd accomplished her goal of discouraging him. "Would you mind taking me home?"

He looked at his drink which all of a sudden seemed uninteresting and walked over to the piano. He stood with his back toward her. He didn't want her to see the disappointment on his face. "Platonic friends?" Johannes whispered under his breath. "As you wish." He tightened his jaw. "I will have Ali drive you home. I'll ride with you."

"I'd prefer to ride alone, Johannes." Lowering her head she said, "I'm sorry Johannes. I didn't want to hurt you like this," she said walking toward the door. Turning around before leaving, she said, "It's for the best."

Johannes stood in front of the piano watching her walk through the front door leaving it wide open. A feeling of sadness came over him as he watched Ali drive her away in the long black limousine. He felt as though he had fallen off of a cliff. How could this happen? The woman he'd desired and nursed back to health had just told him she didn't want a relationship? No woman had ever rejected him. In fact, women manipulated, conned or connived to get his attention, but to flat out reject him like Shana. Never.

One of the things he adored about Shana was her strong-will. He knew she was the type of woman who wouldn't allow him to take her for granted. He lifted his eyebrows and smiled. "She's playing hard to get."

Chapter 7

Johannes pushed back from his dark cherry conference table in the library and began pacing on the plush Persian carpet spread on the dark hardwood floor. He and some of the Council members had worked on the constitution all morning, writing and revising amendments over and over. When the work became exhausting, he took a break and began to think about Shana.

I cannot eat or sleep..., she has me under her spell, he thought. What was it about her that haunted him so? He hated himself for allowing her to control his thoughts. He'd gone off on a tangent. He had to gain control of his emotions and remember why he came to California. He didn't come to chase women. He came to focus on and finishing the document to save his country. As a teenager, after his father ran his girlfriend off, he vowed never to fall in love again. He'd been in love once in his twenty eight years of life. Now twice with Shana. He had to admit. He couldn't stop thinking about Shana since the day he laid eyes on her. He remembered how soft her lips felt and how good she felt in his arms.

He admitted their date last night hadn't gone well. He wasn't angry as much as he was confused. He couldn't understand what made her pull away. And why would she want a platonic friendship with him? He didn't believe for one minute she wanted to be friends—he could feel it in his soul. Something else was going on. Something must have happened to make her feel threatened. What was it, he wondered? What could have happened?

After looking back on how the evening began, he tried to retrace his every action to see if he had said or done anything to insult her. Maybe she felt uncomfortable because of his royal status. That could have intimidated her, he thought. He made a mental note to ask her directly how she felt about his background.

Patience was the key with Shana, he reasoned. He knew she was a passionate woman who held painful secrets within her soul, secrets he intended to resurrect and lay to rest one by one. He told himself he would find a way to make her love him. He refused to let something from her past keep her away from him. One thing he knew for sure was he would not give up on pursuing Shana. He had an idea.

Minutes later, Ababa brought him a sandwich and some fresh mango slices. He still couldn't eat. He picked up his phone and googled "florist."

Shana peered out of her office window overlooking San Francisco Bay and watched the dense fog roll in under the Golden Gate Bridge. She'd grown accustomed to hearing Johannes' voice during his evening telephone calls, inquiring about her health. But for some reason, something inside of her mind blocked his entry into her heart.

She reminded herself over and over a relationship with Johannes would never work, because of his background. As a royal was she supposed to address him as His Imperial Highness Prince Johannes? Really? Everything about his background sounded too unfamiliar, yet she could still hear his silky voice whispering in her ear, and feel the comfort of his strong embrace. She knew deep in her soul she looked for an excuse to push Johannes away. She conjured up other excuses such as her inability to speak his language, even though languages were easy for her to learn. Then she thought about his people. She'd read somewhere that Ethiopia was a closed society. Would his countrymen ever accept her as an American? She didn't want to live her life as an outsider. No way was she going to get involved with Johannes she told herself. She came up with all kinds of excuses why a relationship with him would never work, yet she couldn't deny the feelings in her heart for Johannes.

She picked up her cell phone to call him, and then changed her mind. "If you'd like to make a call, please hang up and call again." Shana turned off her cell phone. She had to pull herself together because she needed to finish those loans sometime today. Why can't I concentrate? Every time I begin to work on my loans, I end up daydreaming about him. She stood up from her desk, picked up her cell phone and called her best friend.

"Hi Lauren, how are you doing?" Shana's voice reflected the way she was feeling, confused.

"I'm fine, Shana, but I can tell by the tone in your voice something is bothering you. What's wrong?"

Shana sat back down and pushed the manila file folder aside on her desk, and rested her face in the palms of her hands. "I guess I need someone to talk to."

Shana felt like crying because her life had been turned upside down since she'd met Johannes. Before she'd met him, her everyday life was lived in her comfort zone. Working overtime during the week, lunch with Lauren and weekends watching the latest Hollywood movies or visiting her aunt. But now she'd gotten glimpses of life with a man who adored her. What was she to think? Her heart was pulling in two different directions—living a life moving up the career ladder at work, or spending time with Johannes, a man who made her feel like a princess. Her mind was in a tangle of confusion.

"Got any plans for lunch?" Shana asked looking out into the foggy bay, twirling her gold pin between her fingers. Sheila came in and brought her a message written on a small yellow post-it note. It was a message from her Aunt Helen. She nodded and smiled at Sheila and continued her conversation with Lauren.

"I don't have any plans for lunch. What do you

have in mind?" Lauren asked.

Shana doodled Johannes' name on the bottom of the post it notes. "Let's go to the Thai restaurant we went to last month. I have something to tell you."

"I'll meet you at noon. This time Shana, please be on time, Okay!"

"I'll be on time."

Shana ended the call and picked up the manila folder on her desk. She spent the rest of the morning working on the loan she should have finished by now.

Shana arrived at the Thai restaurant first. She sat down at a table near the front and waited for Lauren. About ten minutes later she looked up from her menu and saw Lauren waving to her through the window.

"Hey Shana, what's going on?" Lauren asked, walking up to her table.

"My dinner last night with Johannes was a disaster," Shana confessed. "I told him I wasn't interested in pursuing a romantic relationship with him. I told him I wanted us to be platonic friends."

Lauren raised a skeptical brow. "What did he say?"

"Not much. He didn't appear to be angry."

Shana picked up her napkin and wiped her glistening eyes. “Lauren, what is the matter with me? This man has been nothing but a perfect gentleman to me, kind and loving, and look how I treat him. At first I thought I was more grateful than anything. But I spent most of the morning thinking about him and couldn’t concentrate on my work. What’s wrong with me Lauren?”

Lauren looked up from her menu. “Sounds like you’re in love.” She continued to search the menu and said. “The sooner you admit it, the better off you’ll be.” She’d made her selection and closed the menu. Giving Shana a serious look, she said. “Why don’t you at least give him a chance Shana?”

“A chance at what Lauren?”

“A chance to have a second, third, or a fourth date with you.” Her look held a faint sadness. “Haven’t you ever noticed none of your dates have ever gone past the first date?”

Shana’s eyes lit up. “What?”

“You heard me. I’ll repeat it again.” Lauren pronounced every word slowly. “You’ve never dated anyone past the first date, Shana. I noticed this pattern when we were in high school. You always find something wrong with the man before the second date. I think you have a problem with intimacy.”

“Intimacy?” Shana was stunned at Lauren’s

revealing declaration. She never noticed a pattern before, and she never thought she had a problem with intimacy.

"I think you should see him again."

Shana didn't say a word. She thought about Lauren's eye opening statement.

Lauren poured some Jasmine tea into their cups, giving Shana an annoyed look. "I must have hit a nerve."

Shana twisted in her chair and changed the subject. For the rest of the meal, they talked about everything else except Shana's problem. After lunch, they both went back to work. Now Shana understood what was wrong with her. But she didn't know why.

When Shana returned to her office, she opened the double glass doors and gasped. Long-stemmed pink, red and yellow roses displayed in vases sat on every credenza, desk, and counter. Pink and white lilies, and irises of every hue filled the office with a sweet heady bouquet.

Sheila's eyes widened when she saw Shana's shocked expression. She ran from behind her desk to greet Shana. She eagerly handed Shana a small sealed envelope with a card inside. "This came with the first vase of red roses," Sheila smiled. "I put them on your desk."

Shana opened the card and read it. "I'm sorry about last night, please let me make it up to you... Johannes."

Shana's eyes began to water as she walked down the corridor to her office. She opened the door to her office and saw a dozen long-stemmed American Beauty roses in a crystal vase sitting on her desk. She walked over to the bouquet of roses and inhaled deeply. The fragrance of the roses brought Johannes' gentle, caring spirit to her mind. She sat in her chair and cried. She felt guilty about how she had treated him. Lauren was right, she had a problem with intimacy and she should give Johannes a chance. Suddenly she heard her cell phone ring.

"Shana, how are you feeling today?" Johannes asked on the other end of the phone.

Shana leaned forward on her elbows, resting her chin in the palms of her hands as she spoke. . "I'm feeling better Johannes, especially after I received all of those flowers. What about you? How are you feeling today?"

He paused. "I'm fine Shana. I called to apologize about last night. I'm sorry if I offended you. Please..."

"No, Johannes." Shana interrupted. "You didn't offend me one bit. You've been nothing but kind and good to me. It's me." she said softly, reflecting on Lauren's statement during lunch.

Johannes leaned back in his armchair, rubbing his thumb and forefinger against the stubble growing on his handsome face. He felt relieved to hear her open up. He was sure she wouldn't answer his call.

"Thank you for the flowers." She pulled a tissue from a box and wiped her watery eyes.

Johannes felt overwhelmed with her change of heart.

"Listen, I remember what you said last night about action movies."

"Um hmm," Shana replied as she unbuttoned her jacket.

"Well, I found out about this theater in Palo Alto shows nothing but Hollywood action movies. Would you like to go on Friday?"

"Sure," Shana said walking over to her file cabinet to replace the manila folder. "Yes, I'd love to go."

"Fine, then I will pick you up at 7:00 on Friday."

"I'll be ready."

Johannes ended the call, not wanting to press his luck. Shana sounded much better today, he thought. He wanted to give Shana some space. He told himself he would not attempt to kiss her again. She would have to initiate the next kiss. He hoped he would be able to control his burning desire for Shana. She was beautiful and full of pent-up passion—one look at her set his soul on fire. He spent the remainder of the day working on the constitution.

The rest of the week moved quickly for Johannes. He'd met with the Council members every day to work on the constitution. Though he derived much pleasure working on the political document that would change the course of his country, he still couldn't stop thinking about Shana. He waited with great anticipation for his date on Friday night.

Wednesday morning he received a phone call from his friend Sifani at around 8:30 a.m.

"Hello Sifani, it is good to hear from you. How goes everything with you?"

"I'm calling to find out how everything went with our patient. I'm assuming everything went well with her because I haven't heard from you since the accident."

"Sifani, I have been busy working on the amendments. I am almost finished. How is Stephanie?"

"She's fine. In fact, she wanted me to invite you to dinner tonight at our house. Do you have any plans?"

"No, I do not. Dinner sounds good. What time should I arrive?"

"Sevenish?"

"Sounds good." They continued to talk about current events back home and then began to talk about their childhood adventures. Johannes looked forward to the drive to Sifani's home. He had been cooped up with his work for the entire week. He looked forward to the company of his childhood friend.

When Johannes arrived, Stephanie and Sifani both came to the door and greeted him with a big bear hug.

"So, Johannes," Stephanie inquired. "How is your beautiful patient feeling these days?"

Johannes gave Sifani a sideways glance. "She is fine, Stephanie."

"Did you ever find out any information about her? Who is she? Where does she live?"

"Yes, her name is Shana Zachary, she lives in Sausalito and she has an aunt who lives in Sacramento. I had her over for dinner last week. I have a date with her this Friday."

"Well, you must bring her over for us to meet one day."

"Stephanie, maybe you can give me some tips on how to handle American women. You know, how they think and act. I do not understand a lot about them."

"Well, I can tell you one thing. She's probably intimidated by the fact that you're a prince."

"I hope that is not the case."

They all laughed and reminisced about old times.

"So, how is everything going at work Sifani?" Johannes asked.

"Fine."

Stephanie interrupted. "Sifani, he doesn't want to hear about your work. We never finished showing him around the Bay Area."

"All right Stef, whatever you say."

"Do you have plans for the holidays Johannes?" Stephanie asked.

"I don't celebrate Thanksgiving."

"Why don't you celebrate Thanksgiving with us, or at least keep the day open for us to meet Miss

Zachary? We can all go up to our cabin in Lake Tahoe."

"Okay," Johannes agreed.

"Good. It is set. We promise to show your friend a good time."

"It is a tentative date. Remember, I have to ask Shana, she may have other plans with her aunt." Johannes said.

***

Friday came quickly. Johannes and the Council worked all day on the amendments and kept at it until it was time to meet Shana. Johannes was excited about his date with Shana. He also had to face the fact he couldn't allow her to occupy his mind.

He decided to give Ali the night off and drove to Shana's home by himself, with his security following at a unnoticeable distance behind. During the ride, he still couldn't believe how beautiful the area was especially with the towering redwood trees.

At precisely six forty-five, Johannes knocked on Shana's front door. He was a stickler for time, a habit he developed in his military training.

When Shana opened the door, she was pleasantly surprised to see a clean-shaven, brother with a neat haircut, decked out in a brown leather jacket with a faux shearling collar, hunter green trousers and matching green shirt. Johannes looked nothing like a prince. He looked like an average everyday brother.

Shana stepped back with most of her weight on her left leg, crossed her arms and held her chin between her thumb and index finger. "Do I know you?" She greeted him with a light kiss on the lips and invited him to come in.

Shana led him inside. "Let me get my coat and I'll be ready to go."

Johannes' mind began thinking of various lovemaking positions. Her perfect female form looked sexy in her skinny jeans and low cut cashmere sweater.

Johannes waited patiently in the foyer for Shana to gather her jacket and handbag, then they left. When they reached the black Cadillac Escalade, Johannes quickly ran around to open the passenger side for Shana.

Shana slid on her seatbelt and asked, "Johannes, how did you find out about this place? I never heard of it."

"My friends Sifani and Stephanie told me about it."

As Johannes drove along highway 101, he

couldn't stop wondering why Shana had rejected him the other night, and now was welcoming him with open arms. He was determined to find out what made Shana tick.

"Shana, may I ask you a question?"

"Sure."

"Why did you reject me the other night?"

Shana hoped he wouldn't ask her that question because she knew she had a problem with intimacy, but she didn't understand why.

Johannes picked up on her reluctance to answer the question. "You don't have to answer my question if you don't want to. I was curious."

Shana didn't answer him, she looked out the passenger window and said, "Thanks."

Johannes changed the subject because he didn't want to make Shana feel uncomfortable. "Why do you love those Hollywood action movies?"

Shana's eyes lit up reflecting the change in her mood. "I love them because the action holds my attention."

"So what are some of your favorite movies?"

The question was right up Shana's alley. She turned her body slightly toward him. "I love anything by Marvel or DC comics." Shana laughed,

I could keep going on all night.

Johannes smiled, happy with the way their date was going. “You know I could listen to you all night too. Did you know American movie stars are very popular in Africa?”

“What?” Shana asked.

“Yes, they are. People all over the world love Hollywood movies?”

When they arrived at the movie theater, it was seven fifteen. Johannes opened Shana’s door and took her by the hand, walking briskly to the theater. After buying the tickets, he asked her if she wanted some popcorn. They waited in line to get it and then found seats.

After the movie, while driving on the way home, Johannes asked Shana if she would mind if they stopped at Twin Peaks to look at the view of the city. Sifani had told him Twin Peaks was where lovers went to enjoy the view of the bridges, the bays, and lights. Shana, to her surprise found herself agreeing. Johannes thought it was a beautiful sight.

When Johannes parked the car, feelings of apprehension began to overtake Shana. A million questions raced through her mind. She still didn’t understand why she was afraid of intimacy.

Johannes could sense her anxiety. His hand fell

to her shoulder and caressed the texture of her light brown curly hair. "Do not be afraid" he whispered, holding her in his gaze. I wanted to come up here to talk to you."

Shana slowly exhaled. "What do you want to talk about?"

"I was hoping we could continue with the conversation we had on the way to the movies."

Shana leaned her head back on the neck rest and stared blankly into the lights below. "I rejected you the other night because I have a fear of intimacy."

Johannes felt nothing but compassion for Shana when he heard her answer. He reached over and brushed a loose strand of hair from her face and took her hand into his. "Why are you afraid of intimacy?"

"I'm not sure," she said staring through the passenger window. "But I think my problem stems from the death of my parents. I don't allow myself to get intimately close. After the first date my relationships have a pattern of fizzling out." Shana confessed. "I think I rejected you the other night because I'm afraid of allowing you to get too close," she said still looking through the window.

With the tip of his index finger, Johannes turned her head to face him. His eyes were gentle and thoughtful. "You have no reason to fear me Shana?

You are a wonderful woman. I would never do anything to hurt you."

Shana lowered eyes, watching the twinkling lights below as if she would find some answers in them. "I am twenty-five years old and I have never been in a serious relationship Johannes. I have never been in love." She lifted her eyelids and stared into his eyes. "I've never told this to anyone."

Johannes was not surprised at her confession, because back home, young women never had boyfriends. They went straight from their parents' house to their husband's house. "The fact you have never been in love is nothing to be ashamed of Shana."

Shana gave him a surprised look. She was ashamed of treating him badly the other night. She found herself wondering what it would feel like to be in love. "Have you ever been in love Johannes?"

Johannes leaned back in his seat and thought about the girl he'd loved as a teen. "Yes. I've been in love."

"What can you tell me about love, Johannes?"

Johannes' eyes lit up like the San Francisco skyline. He gave Shana a boyish grin. "Love can make a man do crazy things." He leaned over, resting his hand on Shana's hand. "Love can possess a man's mind to the point he would do anything for his beloved." He decided to tell Shana how he felt about her. "You have found a place in my heart Shana. A man cannot tell his heart who to love. A heart has a mind all of its own. All I know is I cannot eat, or sleep. I think about you all of the time."

Shana wanted to face her fear of intimacy. She opened up and told him how she felt about him. "I've been thinking a lot about you too Johannes. I suspect I'm in love with you, but I don't know how to show it."

"I'm happy to hear you've been thinking about me Shana. When you are ready, I will teach you how to love."

"Thanks for being patient with me and my problem Johannes."

"I'm a very patient man Shana," he said staring at her for a long time. He reached out and gently pulled her hand into his, kissing it. Speaking in a calm voice he said, "I'll wait for you as long as necessary." He desperately wanted to get close to Shana, but he knew closeness was not what Shana needed right now. She needed patience and understanding, those two things came easily to him. The more Shana revealed about herself, the more he loved her.

***

The ride to Shana's home was quiet. When

Johannes drove up to her front door, he got out to open the car door for her. She was about to walk inside, when he took her by the arm, turning her to face him. He looked deeply into her eyes and said, "Shana, do not allow fear to control your happiness. Once you let go of your fear of intimacy, you won't have to ask me what it feels like to be in love." He kissed her on the forehead. "I'll wait until you are safely inside before I leave."

Shana walked inside and closed the door softly behind her.

Chapter 8

Three buses made a path down the dry rocky slopes into the city limits of Addis Ababa, Ethiopia. The busloads carried young students on their way to protest and change their lives. The buses lined up in front of the University of Addis Ababa, which stood catty-corner to the Egyptian Embassy and across the street from the renowned Black Lion Hospital, noted for serving Ethiopia's royalty. Numerous sidewalk cafes, libraries, restaurants, and office buildings curved around a large circular garden laced with purple and yellow pansies, forming a pleasant city center.

One by one, the students exited, in single file, off the buses and began walking into the Registrar's Office determined to enroll. The University was too strict in their admission standards.

The students stood in front of the entrance to the Registrar's Office holding protest signs, reminiscent of Little Rock, Arkansas in the early nineteen fifties. The students demanded to be allowed to enroll. A tall, thin armed security guard came up to the leader and demanded they remove themselves from the premises. The leader refused and applied his non-violent tactics by ignoring the threats of the security guard.

After thirty minutes had passed, the military

arrived and began shoving the students, hitting them with Billy clubs. A soldier hit the leader in the head with the long end of his Billy club. The other students were kicked and beaten, but no one was killed.

When Bari heard about the protest, his fears began to surface. Conflicts were getting worse as the days went by. He hoped Johannes was almost finished with the amendments. He decided to call Johannes and discuss the incident in the morning.

***

Johannes slept quietly with a smile on his face. He was almost finished with the first draft of the amendments, and Shana was responding to his advances. Somewhere between a dream and consciousness, he saw images of them lying on a pristine beach making love. In the middle of his dream, he was awakened by the sound of his cell phone.

"What!" He sat up on the bed and grabbed his phone.

"Johannes, it is me, Bari."

He turned on the speakerphone. "Bari!" Johannes said rubbing his face with the palms of his hands. "How are you?"

"I am the same since I spoke to you three days ago."

"Good. I am thankful you have been checking on my father and sisters." Johannes stated as he stood up to stretch.

"They are all fine."

"Good." What is the reason for the call?" Johannes asked as he rubbed his arm while looking for his robe.

"I wanted to let you know about a protest downtown yesterday."

"A protest!" Johannes stopped in his tracks. "Anyone hurt?"

"Thank God, no," Bari said, remembering the report of the beatings.

"What happened?" Johannes asked as he continued to search for his robe.

"Some students tried to enroll in the University today. I believe their ultimate goal was not to register, as much as to bring attention to their plight."

"Did the military come out?"

"Yes."

"What did they do?" Johannes asked.

"They roughed up some of the students, but no one was killed."

"Thank you for keeping me posted, Bari."

"How are the amendments coming?" Bari asked.

"I've been working on them every day since I arrived. I am more than half way finished. It will be a matter of weeks before I'm finished. I will let you know when it gets close to the time because I will need you to help me coordinate a conference with the UN and get a vote in Parliament on the amendments."

"A conference? Votes?"

"Yes. When I get back, I want you to help me set up a UN peacekeeping conference," Johannes replied. "I plan to invite leaders from every major ethnic group in Ethiopia to the conference."

Bari nodded his head, "I will do anything you ask, Johannes."

"I want you to contact and invite all of the leaders to this meeting. Our new constitution will guarantee everyone equal rights under the law."

Bari leaned back in his chair and crossed his legs. "Sounds good."

"Okay, my friend, I will talk to you later."

"Goodbye."

Ali stood listening to Johannes' conversation at

his bedroom door. Ababa saw Ali eavesdropping, but continued with her dusting, acting as though she heard nothing.

Bari's phone call encouraged Johannes to spend more time working on the amendments. But, even a prince only had twenty four hours in a day. He and the Council couldn't work all day and night on the documents. He made it a point to make enough time in the day to deal with his work and his heart, because he could deny neither.

Chapter 9

Lauren called Shana early Saturday morning to inquire about her movie date with Johannes. "Okay. Tell me. How did your date go?"

"Huh?" Shana replied sleepily.

"How did your date go," Lauren asked, bright-eyed.

"Lauren, it is eight o'clock in the morning, why don't you let me call you back?"

"Hold it, wait one minute before you hang up on me. Don't forget we're supposed to go shopping today."

"Oh yeah, you're right" Shana replied with a yawn.

"Why don't we meet for brunch and then we can leave from the restaurant."

"Usual place."

"Of course."

"What time?" Shana asked sleepily.

"Eleven" Lauren dictated.

"Okay."

Shana pulled the covers over her head and went back to sleep. Several hours later, the bright sunlight shined through her bedroom window casting a soft shadow on her face. She looked over at the clock and saw it was ten o'clock. She leaned back on her elbows. The first thought coming into her mind was Lauren. "She's going to kill me," she said to herself. She ran her fingers through her hair, stretched out her arms and wondered what she was going to tell Lauren about her date with Johannes.

She got up, put on her robe, showered and slipped on a pair of camel slacks and an ivory cashmere sweater. As she slipped on her tan suede flats, her cell phone rang. She rushed to answer the call.

"Hello, beautiful, how are you feeling this morning?"

Shana stretched back and fell onto her unmade bed, smiling at the sound of his voice. "I'm feeling a lot better. You have to forgive me; I went off last night. I'm sorry."

"It's nothing. Do you have plans this morning?"

"Yeah, I do, but don't you have to work?"

"I need to take some time off. What about tonight?"

"I don't have any plans for tonight."

"Sifani and Stephanie told me the Dance Theatre of Harlem will be performing in Los Angeles all week."

"Who are Sifani and Stephanie?"

"They are some friends of mine; you will meet them later. The Dance Theatre of Harlem will be performing the "Firebird" tonight. Aren't they your favorite dance group?"

"Yes, it is."

"Want to go?"

A big smile crossed her face. She felt happy, not because she could see the DTH, but because Johannes had taken the time to listen to her.

"The first show starts at eight. We need to be at the airport by six. I will pick you up at five.

"Five O'clock, I'll be ready."

Shana showered, dressed and pulled her rust suede coat from the closet and went to meet Lauren at their favorite restaurant. She told Lauren all about her date with Johannes. Lauren felt slightly disturbed when Shana told her how the date ended.

"But, guess what?" Shana said.

"What?"

"I have another date with him tonight; he's taking me to Los Angeles to see the Dance Theater of Harlem."

"You mean you're going to go out with him again? I thought you would reject him because he's a prince or find something wrong with him.

"Thanks to you, I'm trying to work on my pattern," Shana replied.

Shocked at her friend's change of heart, Lauren stated, "I'm proud of you Shana. Maybe there is hope for you after all. I've never seen you go out with anyone more than once." Lauren said. "Remember when I introduced you to several of Jamal's friends?"

"Yes. I remember them."

"You found fault in both of them." Lauren said as she finished the last of her quiche.

"I'm sorry Lauren."

"You should be sorry."

They drove to Neiman Marcus in the Union Square shopping district in San Francisco. Shana felt confident about her anticipated promotion. She decided to splurge a little. Whenever she spent money, visions of her aunt pointing her finger in her face, telling her to save up for a rainy day, plagued her mind. Shana already had a substantial savings account, stocks and bonds, an IRA and mutual funds and owned her townhouse.

Once inside the store, Shana gave out orders like a lieutenant. "Okay, we are going to split up temporarily, but let's meet back at the cosmetics counter in one hour."

Lauren agreed.

Lauren went to the shoe department, and Shana went straight to the designer boutiques. She was looking for a silk blouse she'd seen in Vogue magazine several weeks ago. She found it and took it to the dressing room. It fit perfectly on her size six figure. After coming out of the dressing room, Shana gave the blouse and her credit card to the saleswoman. Now, one more stop. She found an understated black pantsuit that would look great with some black ankle boots she'd recently purchased.

It was two o'clock when Shana finished shopping. She was satisfied with her purchases and realized it was time to meet Lauren at the cosmetics counter. She took the escalator down to the first floor and saw Lauren standing at the cosmetics counter, purchasing a lip gloss.

Shana snuck up behind Lauren, "Hey. You ready?"

"Sure, I'm finished," Lauren replied, testing her new lip gloss."

"Yeah, I better get home and prepare for my date with Johannes tonight."

Shana was pleased with her progress. She was ready for her second date with Johannes.

***

"Hello beautiful," the smooth sexy voice said on her cell phone.

"Hi, Johannes," Shana replied cheerfully.

"Are you getting ready?"

Shana kicked her shoes off and slid onto her oversized white leather sofa. "Yes, I am."

"Okay, see you at five."

Shana carried her shopping bag into her bedroom. She chose to wear an ivory sleeveless spandex dress, with an ivory mohair jacket. She accessorized her outfit with diamond stud earrings, an ivory evening bag and pumps. She let her long curly brown hair hang down her back loose and full.

When Johannes arrived, he was stunned once again at Shana's attractiveness. They left promptly at five. Ali drove them to the San Francisco Airport where they and Johannes's security boarded a private plane. They arrived at the theater forty-five minutes later. Johannes handed the attendant the tickets. The attendant tore the tickets in half and returned them to Johannes.

"Do you mind if I keep the ticket stubs? I collect them for souvenirs." Shana explained.

Johannes handed her the ticket stubs and she tucked them into her wallet.

The lights dimmed as they walked inside the auditorium. A prince soared into the air across the elaborately decorated stage and danced his way into Shana's heart.

When they arrived back at Shana's house, Johannes walked her to the door. He pulled the collar of Shana's jacket closer around her neck to ward off the chill of the evening air. Taking her hand, he softly caressing it. "It has been relaxing spending the evening with you, Shana."

She looked first at his hand caressing hers, and then into his eyes. "Thank you, Johannes. I'm happy you thought of me when you heard about the dance group."

"It was nothing," Johannes said. He raised Shana's hand to his mouth, kissing it gently.

Shana felt butterflies in the pit of her stomach at the touch of his lips on her hand. Memories of their last kiss crossed her mind as he said his good-byes. Shana waited for him to kiss her, but he did not.

He gently released her hand and stepped a little closer. “Shana, I want to see you tomorrow night.” He said as he touched the side of her face gently.

Shana waited for him to kiss her. She remembered what Lauren had said about her fear of intimacy. At that moment, she decided to stand up to her fears.

Johannes asked her again. “Are you available tomorrow night?”

Shana stared into his handsome face and said, “Yes.”

“Then I’ll see you then?”

***

The next morning, Johannes sat at the large conference table in the library surrounded by ten of his key representatives. Today, he wanted to add a provision to ban discrimination against all ethnicities in employment, education, and in places of public accommodations.

Two Council members stood up and voiced support for part of his provision. They rejected the provision guaranteeing equal access to places of public accommodations to all citizens. With images fresh in his mind of the students attempting to enroll in the University, Johannes argued back and forth with the two dissenting representatives on this issue for hours. He pressed hard for this provision because it could be used to protect peaceful protesters and voters from brutal military attacks. He also wanted to authorize the Courts to have jurisdiction over cases involving federal laws, trans-regional issues, and issues of national importance.

After hours of arguing, Johannes persuaded one of the two Council members to accept his provision. The other member, an avid separationist, indicated his intention to keep the provision bottled up indefinitely in Parliament.

Johannes thought about all of the border wars Ethiopia had suffered with its neighbors for centuries. He stood up and walked around the table, making a passionate plea to the one dissenting Council member. He looked him dead in the eye.

"As you all know, Ethiopia is divided into ethnically based regions made up of similar looking people. The world sees us as brothers fighting brothers. We should start thinking of ourselves as brothers, and stop thinking like separationists." Johannes stopped. "I'm finished for the day. We can continue with this discussion tomorrow."

***

At seven thirty in the evening, Shana looked through her glass oven door and saw the tips of the trout had turned brown. The aroma of fresh ginger lingered in the air teasing her senses and the heat from the oven warmed her cold body. After making a salad, she folded together some cooked white rice, chopped dates, grated ginger, nuts, and a touch of sugar. Now this is a masterpiece, she thought. Shana prided herself on being a good cook.

She'd taken a shower earlier and styled her hair in a ponytail. Now everything was under control in the kitchen. She quickly retreated into her bedroom pulling out a white silk loose-fitting tunic and white leggings. She accessorized her outfit with large silver hoop earrings.

"Oh no, I forgot to set the table." She went into the dining room and pulled out two place settings from her buffet and placed them on the dining room table. Suddenly, she heard raindrops beating against her dining room window. It would have to rain now. She remembered seeing dark clouds earlier in the morning when looked through the dining room window.

She finished dressing, and then came back into the living room and pulled out her chess set. She wanted to check Johannes skills. No one had ever beaten her at chess. Not even the countless members of the chess team in college.

After she'd set up the chess board on the coffee table, she turned on her Bose docking station and played some music she'd downloaded last week. Suddenly the doorbell rang.

She cleared the butterflies from her stomach and opened the door.

Johannes stood under a large black umbrella, in the downpour of rain. He looked like the epitome of casual elegance in a brown leather jacket and black Levis jeans. Shana liked the way he looked in his casual clothing. She immediately felt comfortable.

“Hi, Johannes, come inside.” She flashed him a smile and kissed him lightly on the lips.

“Hello, Shana,” Johannes replied. He pressed a button to lower his umbrella and then stepped across the threshold. He pulled a bouquet of red roses from behind his back and handed them to Shana.

“They’re beautiful. Thank you,” Shana replied, admiring the long-stemmed flowers. She had developed a true appreciation for flowers when she played in her aunt’s garden as a child. “Red is one of my favorite colors.”

“I’m glad you like them,” Johannes said. “We grow a lot of roses back home and export them to Europe.” He made a mental note that red was one of her favorite colors.

“Here, let me take your coat,” she said, taking the wet garment from his hands, and hanging it on a coat rack in the corner of the foyer.

Shana led him into the living room. “Have a seat, while I put these in some water. I’ll be with you in a moment.”

“Shana, do you want me to light your fireplace while you arrange the flowers?”

“Sounds great.”

By the time Shana returned with the flowers in a crystal vase, the fireplace was starting to warm up the place. Sapphire found herself a nice cozy spot right in front of the fire.

Johannes patted the cushion on the sofa next to him. “Come, sit by me for a minute and relax.” Sapphire gave him a jealous look when she saw her mistress sit next to Johannes.

“Would you like some wine?” Shana asked before sitting next to him.

“I will take mine with dinner,” Johannes replied calmly. He picked up Shana’s hand and rubbed it gently. “I have something I want to ask you tonight,” Johannes stated seriously.

Sapphire jumped up on the sofa and squirmed her way onto Shana’s lap. Shana put her down.

“Can it wait until after dinner? I’m famished, I haven’t eaten all day. Are you ready to eat?”

“Yes, My Dove.” Johannes replied.

“My Dove?” Shana’s eyes lit up. She’d never heard anyone use such a term of endearment before.

She liked it. “I hope you like seafood?” Shana asked.

“I love seafood.”

Shana took his hand into hers and led him to his seat at the dining room table. She fixed him an average-size portion. She didn’t want to assume he would care for her cooking. She sat at the table and was surprised to see Johannes ate his meal quickly with a healthy appetite while displaying perfect table manners. He’d learned to eat quickly while he was in the military.

“Shana, you are an extremely good cook,” he said between bites. “These spices remind me of Middle Eastern cooking.”

Shana smiled at the compliment. “I copied the recipe from an online cookbook. I have more if you want.”

“I cannot eat another bite. Thank you.” Johannes replied as he ate the last bits of fish lingering on the skeleton.

The delicious meal and her company were satisfying to Johannes. He wanted to reach over and kiss Shana right now, but he remembered his vow.

Shana saw him staring at her and could feel what he was thinking. She looked down at Sapphire rubbing against her leg.

Johannes was glad Shana couldn't read his mind.

After they finished, Johannes stayed in his chair and started a conversation because Shana had affected him to the degree that he was embarrassed to stand. He enjoyed Shana's home-cooked meal. He even liked her spoiled cat Sapphire, but most of all he liked how comfortable he felt around Shana.

"What was it like growing up here in California? Did you have many friends?"

"No, actually, I was a pretty lonely kid." Shana stated. "I remember when I was in the seventh grade, I had two good friends—Brittany and Tiffany. I remember when Brittany told me I should not be friends with Tiffany because she was her enemy. Brittany still doesn't know how she hurt me. She forced me to choose between them both. But I couldn't."

"What did you do?" Johannes asked.

"I took my aunt's advice." She paused. "I never let my right hand know what my left hand was doing."

Johannes laughed. "You are a true diplomat."

"My aunt taught me to base my friendships on a person's inner character."

Johannes raised his eyebrows and leaned

forward. “Then I have a question to ask you.”

“What is it?” Shana gave him an inquisitive look.

“How do you feel about my inner character?”

Shana thought about his good characteristics and wondered about his flaws. “Don’t you have any flaws?”

“Flaws. Yes, I have many.”

“Tell me some.”

“I can be inflexible at times. I also don’t like to be controlled.”

“So you admit you are a control freak?”

“Control freak? No.” He thought about how he had bucked his father’s controlling behavior. “I don’t like other people forcing their will on me. I tend to become confrontational and inflexible when people try to control me.” Johannes looked up to find himself under Shana’s speculative scrutiny.

Shana closed her eyes. “I have my reservations about our different backgrounds.” One by one Shana began listing their differences.

“Are you finished?” Johannes asked, moving the fish skeleton around on his plate.

Shana thought of it. “Yes, I’m finished.”

"I have this to say about our differences. You focus on our differences. I focus in on our similarities. I truly believe we have more in common than you may think. I learned a long time ago a broken heart does not feel good to anyone, nor does an empty stomach. When you look at me, you see my crown, my language, my culture. When I look at you, all I see is the woman I love. I hope one day you can see me as the man you love."

Shana sat quietly thinking about Johannes' statement. She knew every word he said was true. Maybe he needed to say the words out loud for them to sink into her head. "You're right Johannes." I'm sorry for rejecting you because of our differences."

Johannes smiled. "You are forgiven."

When their conversation came to a close, Shana could not hide the large yawn escaping her. She was a bit tired from the long day, but Johannes' had changed her attitude and she wanted the date to continue. She began clearing the table, and to her surprise Johannes began to help.

"You don't have to do that."

"But, I want to Shana."

"Okay. Thanks."

After they finished the dishes, Shana made coffee and led the way to the living room where they sat in front of the roaring fire.

Shana lay her head against the sofa. Johannes slid his arm around her shoulder and pulled her closer to him. Shana didn't object.

"Now, as I was saying before dinner."

"Oh yes, you had something to tell me."

Johannes corrected her. "Correction. I have something to ask you."

"What is it?"

"Shana, I want you to see me exclusively."

Shana's almond-shaped eyes widened. "You mean like be your girlfriend?"

"Yes. I am asking you to be my girlfriend?"

Shana thought about it for a moment. "I don't know if I'll make a good girlfriend Johannes because I've never had a boyfriend before."

"Yes. You mentioned that before."

That night at Twin Peaks, Johannes had unknowingly unlocked Shana's mind, heart, and soul, paving the way for her first serious relationship. She was aware of her feelings and no longer afraid of intimacy. Shana watched Johannes look her over seductively.

Every time his gaze met hers, Shana's heart turned over in response. His glance slid rapidly over her silky blouse as if he was photographing her naked body with his eyes. Her heart jolted, and her pulse pounded at his suggestive gaze.

Since that first kiss, she'd dreamt of feeling his strong arms around her body and his moist lips kissing hers. Something masculine yet gentle about him made her feel comfortable in his presence. She moved closer.

He encircled her midriff with his arms while remembering his vow to let her initiate their next kiss. He waited patiently, for her to kiss him.

Shana could feel his hot breath on her neck as he roused her passion. She parted her lips and kissed him with a hunger that belied her outward calm. The caress of his lips on her mouth set her body aflame. Her mind relived the velvety warmth of that first kiss. Johannes showered kisses on her lips, and along her jaw and neck.

There was a dreamy intimacy to their kiss now that felt satisfying and new to Shana. After five minutes of kissing, he left her mouth burning with fire. Between kisses, Shana said, "we better stop while we're ahead, Johannes."

"I never want to stop kissing you Shana," Johannes whispered in her ear.

Looking into his eyes, Shana said, "Thank you

for helping me face my fear of intimacy."

Suddenly, a deep roar of thunder rumbled across the sky, vibrating the earth, followed by a loud crackle of lightning illuminating the sky in a brilliant white glow. Storms evoked emotions in Shana like nothing else in the world. Johannes felt a wave of tension sweep through Shana's body. He put his arms around her shoulders. She released herself from his embrace and walked over to the dining room window. She saw a willow tree flailing in the wind and quickly closed the drapes.

Johannes walked over and stood behind her, rubbing her back in a soothing motion. Another great boom of thunder crashed across the sky. Shana closed her eyes and turned around to face Johannes as the ugly memories of the tragic night crossed her mind. Mental pictures of her parents' dead bodies floating in the Pacific Ocean flashed through her mind.

"I never told you, but…" her voice became edgy, "it stormed like this that night."

"What night?" Johannes asked.

"You wouldn't understand," she said.

"Try me." Johannes said, holding her stiff body in his embrace. "I cannot leave you like this. Why don't you let me sleep on the sofa tonight? This weather is too dangerous for me to drive through."

Shana knew that he was right. She wouldn't drive in weather like this.

Johannes walked with Shana to her bedroom and sat next to her on the bed. His heart sank as he watched her lie down and ball up into a fetal position. He lowered himself onto the bed and nestled himself behind her body. He whispered in her ear. "Tell me what happened," he said, caressing the side of her face with the back of his hand.

Shana spoke in the darkness. "My parents had taken a vacation to Hawaii for their second honeymoon during the summer of my eighth birthday. On their way back home, a violent storm overtook the jet engine in the DC-10, causing the airplane to plunge into the Pacific Ocean, killing all of the passengers. I hadn't seen my parents all summer and was looking forward to picking them up with my aunt at the airport." Shana paused for a moment and then turned around to face Johannes.

Johannes listened attentively. "Go on," while stroking her back.

"When we arrived at the airport, the airlines informed everyone over a loud speaker that the airplane had crashed into the Pacific Ocean and was pending an investigation. The plane crash was all over the news. I never saw my parents after that storm. Part of me died that night. I withdrew into myself. I believed if I allowed myself to love anyone that they would be taken away from me like my parents."

After a few seconds, Johannes whispered into her ear. "You're wrong Shana. I love you, and I will never leave you. Give me a chance, I'll show you," he said.

After she had fallen asleep in his arms, he drifted into a deep sleep. He left early the next morning after the storm blew over.

Chapter 10

Although Shana hadn't slept well through the storm, she had to admit that Johannes' presence comforted her greatly. Before coming to work, she managed to pull herself together and get to the office on time. All she could think about was Johannes, and how he wouldn't leave her during the storm. He would never know how much she appreciated that.

She immediately began returning phone calls. Sheila had left a message marked urgent from Senor Latorre on her desk. Shana returned the call.

"Buenos Dias, La Oficina del Senor Latorre," his secretary said with a deep Spanish accent.

Shana switched her linguistic gears and began speaking in Spanish.

"Yes, my name is Shana Zachary, I'm with the U.S. Foreign Aid Commission and I am returning Senor Latorre's call."

"Si, I will get him for you right away," the secretary replied.

Shana could hear loud voices in the background. Moments later Senor Latorre answered.

“Buenos Dias, Senorita Zachary.”

“Good morning, Senor Latorre. I’m returning your call.”

“Si, Senorita Zachary. My country would like to invite you to an initiation ceremony for our new refinery in Mexico. Since you played a major part in the success of our oil discovery here, we thought it would be appropriate for you to cut the ceremonial ribbon.”

Shana felt flattered with his offer. She’d traveled to countries many times and participated in such events. But this was special to her because she had taken a speculative risk when writing the loan package. She had no idea Central Mexico would find as many fertile oil fields as they had.

“Yes, Senor Latorre, I will be glad to participate in the ceremony. When do you plan to hold the ceremony?”

“Next Thursday at noon.”

“Next Thursday is kind of quick for me to make travel arrangements,” Shana said as she twirled a pencil between her fingers.

“Travel arrangements have already been made,” Senor Latorre replied.

“Okay, I will see you on Thursday.”

As soon as Shana ended the call she went into Mr. Withers office and told him about the invitation.

He leaned back in his chair with his belly bulging over his belt. “Yes, I know all about it, Shana. I was keeping it as a surprise. You have performed extremely well with this Mexican deal. I am giving you a month-long sabbatical with pay. Take a friend if you like. You know, Ms. Zachary, your career is about to take off with lightning speed when you return. I never forgot what you told me about your interest in working abroad. You will be doing a lot of it shortly. I hope you can keep up.”

“Wow!” was all Shana could say. She needed this sabbatical because she’d been working long hours for months at a time. She had to call Lauren and Johannes and let them know about this. She picked up her cell phone and invited Lauren to come with her to Mexico.

“Hi, Lauren, how are you doing?”

“Oh, I’m fine.”

“So what are you doing tonight?”

“I’m going to dinner with my knucklehead boyfriend.”

Shana paused, “anything wrong?”

“No. Typical relationship problems. You have

no idea how lucky you are to have Johannes as a boyfriend."

"I know how lucky I am. Listen, my agency is sending me to Mexico."

"When are you leaving?"

"Next week. I have an extra ticket for you if you want to come with me?"

"Seriously! Of course, I want to come. How did you get the extra ticket?"

"One of the fringe benefits of my job."

Lauren immediately began brushing up on her high school Spanish, which she spoke now and then with her friend Maria.

Next, Shana dialed Johannes' number.

Johannes arrived at his home at 5:30 in the morning feeling tired. He slept until about nine, then got up to work on the constitution. Suddenly his cell phone rang.

"Hi," Shana said in an upbeat voice.

"Hi yourself," Johannes replied smiling. He politely excused himself from the meeting and walked into another room for some privacy. "How are you feeling this morning?" He asked.

"I'm okay. Sorry about last night."

"It is nothing, I hope you understand I couldn't leave you."

"Thank you," Shana replied. "I have some good news."

"What?"

"I've been invited to participate in a ceremony in Mexico. Remember when I told you about the loan I put together for the Mexican government?"

"Yes. I remember."

"Well, they have invited me to cut the ribbon at the initiation ceremony for their new refinery."

"You're lucky," Johannes said, walking over to the terrace looking into the courtyard. "How long will you be away?"

"For about a week," Shana replied. "Lauren is going to come with me. I would invite you, but I know you have a lot of work to do."

"Yes, you are right. I will miss you Shana, but I hope you have a good time. You deserve it."

"Thanks."

"When are you leaving?"

"Wednesday."

"Maybe we can have dinner when you get

back." Johannes wanted to focus on putting the final touches on the amendments. He didn't have a plan to tell Shana he would be leaving for Ethiopia within thirty days. He needed to come up with a plan before she returned.

"Sounds great," Shana said. "Talk to your later."

"Okay, Shana. I'll see you when you get back."

***

Hot and humid air attacked Shana's nostrils, as she and Lauren walked down the steel staircase from the Aero Mexico jet.

Senor Latorre stepped out of a Mercedes Benz wearing a white summer suit and a Panama straw hat. He was a small-boned middle-aged man with dark curly hair and handsome features. His face was clean shaven except for a thin mustache. He walked up to Shana and introduced himself while keeping a sharp eye on Lauren. "Good afternoon ladies. I am Senor Latorre. I'm pleased to meet you."

Shana smiled and held out her hand to shake his.

After shaking her hand, he led them to his car and said, "You know it is siesta time now," he said smiling at Shana and Lauren through pristine white teeth.

"Yes, you're right. In the afternoon, people leave their jobs for siesta and then return to work in the early evening." Shana told Lauren.

He smiled at Shana. "Your understanding of my culture is impressive." He waited to hear something knowledgeable from Lauren.

"You have to excuse me," Lauren said giving him an exhausted look. "A man was sitting behind me snoring loudly for the entire flight. But Shana slept like a baby."

Senor Latorre laughed. "I'm sorry that you had such an unpleasant flight," he said opening the car door for Shana and Lauren.

During the ride, Senor Latorre made small talk, intentionally avoiding anything remotely related to business. "I want you to feel like you're on holiday. After all, you've made me a popular man." He said, pointing out and explaining famous landmarks.

The driver drove them to the Contessa Americana Hotel, an airy, elegant building with high ceiling fans, white marble floors, and lush green palms scattered everywhere. Senor Latorre held his hand out for the ladies to help them get out of the limousine. He walked with them to the registration desk and spoke in a commanding voice. "These women are my guests. Please give them anything they want." He turned to Shana. "Please be my guests at a cocktail party this evening, given in your honor, Senorita Zachary."

Shana accepted the invitation.

He snapped his fingers, and two bellboys appeared out of nowhere escorting Shana and Lauren to their spacious rooms, where they rested for the rest of the day.

At seven o'clock, Senor Latorre stood at the entrance of the ballroom flanked by Shana and Lauren. The room was packed with dignitaries and officials, all forming a receiving line. Senor Latorre introduced Shana and Lauren, who both looked ravishing. Some men shook their hands while some kissed their hands. Lauren gave Shana a questioning look when a man kissed her hand a little too long. Shana returned Lauren's look with a smile. Lauren remembered Shana telling her to be careful because Latin men could be very charming.

Shana and Lauren sat at a table with Senor Latorre. As the evening went on, Shana noticed Senor Latorre couldn't keep his eyes off of Lauren. Shana was shocked to see them both dancing all night. She made a note to ask Lauren how she felt about Senor Latorre's attraction to her later on.

The next day, the ceremony went well. By the end of the week Shana couldn't get her mind off of Johannes, she missed him terribly. She couldn't wait until she returned home. She noticed that Lauren and Senor Latorre, or Carlos, as Lauren had corrected her, weren't helping matters at all with their carrying on. Lauren had told Shana she and her boyfriend had broken up before she left.

Falling in love was something new to Shana.

She didn't think she had it in her. But Lauren was right when she told Shana to admit she was in love with Johannes.

They arrived in San Francisco at 7:30 Friday evening. Johannes picked them up from the airport. When Shana saw Johannes, she gave him a big kiss and told him everything about her trip.

Johannes could see Shana was tired from the long trip. "What do you have planned for tomorrow?"

She looked at him with hooded eyes and said, "sleep."

Good, he thought. He encouraged her to sleep on Saturday because he had a big day planned for them on Sunday.

After Johannes had dropped them off, Shana took a shower and immediately fell asleep. She slept all day Saturday due to jet lag.

Early Sunday morning Johannes began preparing for the day. He had dreamt about kissing Shana all night long. He had missed her terribly in one short week and knew he never wanted to be away from her again. Johannes knew Shana loved the outdoors. He made plans to drive down the coast to Carmel and back to the Napa Valley wine country. Their trip would end with dinner at restaurant in Napa Valley. He'd read about Poppy Hill restaurant in a travel magazine.

He smiled at his plan; he was romantic at heart. He knew Shana would love his plan or at least enjoy the scenic drive. He couldn't wait any longer. He dialed her number.

"Hello, Shana, how do you feel this morning?"

Shana yawned, "I feel great, what about you?"

"I feel energized. What do you think? Are you ready to get out and get some fresh air?"

"Yes, I think it would be nice."

"Okay, I'll pick you up at nine o'clock sharp."

Nine o'clock came quickly for them both. Johannes picked up Shana and complimented her on how lovely she looked in her yellow anorak jacket and black ribbed leggings. He had given Ali the day off because he wanted to spend some time completely alone with Shana, and he didn't want any distractions. He also hadn't liked the way Ali had stared at Shana on several occasions.

They drove down California's great coastal highway, talking and enjoying the breathtaking views of the Pacific Ocean. Shana hadn't noticed until now the luxurious ride of his Cadillac SUV.

"Do you want to hear some music?" She asked.

"Yes, I do," Johannes replied.

"Do you mind if I turn on the radio?"

"No, go ahead."

She pushed the button and turned the knob to a station playing old school rap. She had many questions she wanted to ask Johannes about himself. She knew he was a special man and wanted to find out more about him.

After an hour, Shana asked Johannes if they could get out and stretch. He saw a beach ahead and decided he would take the exit. He pulled the car over and opened Shana's door. Shana stood up and stretched her long legs pressing her shoes against the damp white sand.

The crisp autumn breeze chilled Shana's face. Her hair blew wildly in the wind as she walked toward the beach facing the crashing waves.

Johannes' white windbreaker whipped in the wind as he leaned against the passenger door watching Shana's curvy figure through his Rayban sunglasses. After locking the car, he caught up with Shana. They both removed their shoes and walked hand in hand on the beach following a group of long-beaked sandpipers picking their way through the sand. The scent of marine air prepared their minds for the soothing conversation they were about to have.

Johannes stood on the shore looking out into the distance while Shana threw pebbles into the ocean.

“Something wrong?” Shana asked softly.

“No,” he answered. The endless Pacific Ocean seemed to blend right into the fiery Sun, shining on his handsome face.

A seagull loud cry crowded out the sound of the crashing waves. Shana heard voices of a father and a small son laughing down the beach.

“Johannes, you never told me about your life as a boy growing up?”

Johannes never talked about his childhood with anyone, but with Shana it didn’t matter. He wanted her to know everything about him. He also enjoyed listening to the sound of her soothing voice.

“Johannes?” Shana prompted.

“I’m sorry, what did you ask?”

“What was your life like when you were growing up?”

“Privileged,” he replied abruptly.

Shana stood still, listening to the bitterness in his voice. “Privaledge seems to bother you.”

“Yes, it does.”

“Why?” Shana asked softly.

“Because I never wanted to live a privileged

life. I have seen firsthand how a few people can ruin a country."

"You shouldn't feel bad. You couldn't help it you were born into privilege."

"Yes, I know, but back home, things are much different than here. We are a very traditional lot. We live in a closed system, under a very old class system that separates us."

Shana kicked some sand off of her feet. "You haven't said much about your mother. What was she like?"

Johannes turned to Shana with a sharp look and replied, "My mother relied on my father for everything, even for her thinking. She is why I am attracted to independent women."

He looked down at his waterlogged footprint in the sand and said in a pained voice, "Before she died, she begged me to renounce my political philosophy. To ease her suffering, I told her I would consider it. But, I was determined to change our political system, not myself. She died thinking I had changed myself. My father was very angry at me for a long time because he knew I had not changed."

Shana drew a circle in the sand with the tip of her finger. "Tell me more about your family? How many sisters and brothers do you have?"

“I have two sisters, no brothers. Yasmeen is unmarried and still at home, and Sidha, my older sister, is married.”

“Have you ever loved a woman?” Shana asked. It took Johannes a while to respond.

“Yes,” he replied with a disturbing look in his eye. “Her name was Zahra, my childhood sweetheart. My father forbade me to marry her because of her ethnicity. She and her mother moved into our staff house and worked as servants when I was sixteen. Traditionally male heirs are betrothed to their future wife on their sixteenth birthday and given the public title of Prince, which is suffixed by their birth name. On my sixteenth birthday, I defied my parents and told them I wanted to choose my own wife. I told them I wanted to marry Zahra.”

“My father said such a union would be unacceptable. I thought it was unfair to be denied marriage with a woman on the basis of those rules. A year later she died of typhoid fever. Then I went away to attend Harvard.”

Shana secretly admired Johannes for standing up to his parents. But it also showed her he could be inflexible, not a good trait for a marriage partner. Now that she’d heard of his flaws, she believed he wasn’t perfect after all.

Johannes grabbed Shana’s hand. “Come on, I’ll race you to the end of the pier.”

Shana brushed some sand off of her leggings, "Okay, what does the winner get."

Johannes scanned her body giving her a mischievous grin.

"I set myself up for that one." She called out. "On your mark, get set, go!"

They both sprinted down the beach. Johannes slowed down and let Shana reach the pier before he did.

"I love the water," she said after she reached the pier. She took his hand and began walking toward the shore. The water and sand drifted up her tingling feet.

Johannes looked at her. "I know you love the water. You live by the water, you work by water, and you seem to come alive when you are around water. I could safely say you love water." He took her shoes from her hand. "Here, let me carry these."

After they walked a few hundred feet from the car, they came to a large black porous rock near the edge of the shore. Shana climbed it and sat on its apex. Looking down at Johannes' handsome face.

One corner of his mouth was pulled into a slight smile. He pulled Shana down from the rock and closer to him, burying his face in her hair. He began kissing her temple, cheek, neck, and then her mouth.

Shana kissed him back seductively.

Johannes gave her a serious look while he absorbed what he was feeling. He wanted her to come with him to Ethiopia. He wanted to marry her, but now was not the time to ask her. He took Shana's hand and began walking back to the car.

Johannes drove up the coast, past San Francisco to the Napa Valley where they stopped at a winery called Underwood Hills Winery. They went in for a short wine tasting before dinner. They both tasted a dark red Cabernet. Since Shana loved the wine, Johannes purchased several bottles for her. Later on, Johannes saw the restaurant he'd been looking for from the winery. He pulled up to the Poppy Hill restaurant next door and they both walked inside for an early dinner.

Shana turned to Johannes and smiled. "This has been a real relaxing day. I truly enjoyed the time we spent together."

Johannes felt overjoyed by Shana's compliment. He saw a piano in the corner of the restaurant. He beckoned the manager to come. The manager introduced herself as Briana Underwood, the owner of the restaurant. Johannes slipped Briana some money and asked if she would allow him play a song on the piano. The owner smiled. "Of course. Be my guest." She handed back his money and led him to the piano.

Shana had no idea Johannes was a classically

trained pianist. He sat at the piano and began to play the theme from Tchaikovsky's "Sleeping Beauty." Shana's eyes began to glisten at the smooth melody of the song, and Johannes' hidden talent.

When Johannes returned to the table, Shana smiled and kissed him on the lips. "Your music sounded beautiful, Johannes."

"I played what I feel in my heart for you." The owner came over and complimented Johannes and offered him a job. A couple was sitting at the next table and complimented Johannes as well. They enjoyed the rest of the evening dining on Low Country cuisine and drinking one of the bottles of wine they'd purchased at the winery.

Later in the evening at Shana's doorstep, Johannes said his good-byes. He was about to leave when Shana said, "Wait!"

She didn't have to say another word. Johannes knew what she wanted. He walked back to the porch where Shana leaned against the door, and slowly moved close to her. His warm, moist lips met and parted hers in a slow sensuous kiss. He was intoxicated with her. Shana fell limp into his embrace. She felt lost in a state of bewilderment, as her heart experienced a level of emotion she'd never known. He left her mouth tingling and slowly began moving down her neck. Shana winced at the heat of his tongue as his hot kisses claiming her neck.

After the long slow kiss, Shana stood dazed in

her doorway, lost in another world. Her eyes fluttered open after she came down from the high. In the middle of the crisp autumn, she felt soft and warm as a summer breeze inside her core. Never in her life had she felt this way about a man. All she knew was how much of a fool she had been for not taking Lauren's advice earlier in her life. She wanted Johannes; she wanted him more than anything in the world. She wanted more of his hot, dreamy kisses and his loving ways, and every good feeling he had to offer. She wrapped her arm around his neck. "Johannes, remember the other day when you asked me to see you exclusively?"

His eyes lit up. "Yes, My Dove."

"I never gave you an answer." She paused between kisses. "My answer is…, Yes."

Johannes felt ecstatic. "Shana, you do not know how happy you have made me." He said with a serious look. He was determined to do everything in his power to make Shana happy. He kissed her good night, and she watched him until he got into his SUV. She smiled and waved, then walked inside.

Later in the evening Shana prepared a steaming hot bath. She soaked in the tub with her thoughts drifting on and off of her day with Johannes. She couldn't stop thinking about him playing the piano. She dreamed about Johannes until it was time to get out of the tub. She slipped on a silk gown, set the alarm clock, and slid into bed.

Chapter 11

Celine Dubois looked down at the dazzling San Francisco skyline from her Presidential Suite window atop the Mark Hopkins Hotel. The spectacular Bay Bridge with its light show served as a dramatic backdrop to the hotel's impressive interior surroundings. Her svelte body, elegantly clad in a fitted Chanel suit, was the epitome of the female form. She flung her hair extensions swiftly around from the picture window to face Ali, who sat in a black Italian leather chair. She stared at Ali. "So, you are sure; this woman is spending more time with Johannes?"

"Yes. I am. Three days ago, I drove Prince Johannes, to the airport to pick her up."

"Well, I guess we will have to resort to drastic measures once again. That woman has another thing coming if she thinks she can steal my Johannes."

From afar, thirty-two-year-old Celine Dubois was a very attractive woman, but up close she had bad skin and deep crow's feet around her eyes. She grew up poor in France after her parents migrated from Martinique. After her father died, her mother became a widow and struggled to make ends meet for herself and her three children. Celine's life was hard. She had to struggle for everything.

At seventeen she'd met an African American basketball player while she visited her home in the Caribbean. Six months later, he married her. He gave her everything money could buy. Every day she woke up earlier than him to apply her makeup. She didn't want him to see her facial flaws. But he died of a heart condition a year later. At twenty-five, Celine found herself with several million dollars she'd invested, making her an independently wealthy woman.

She hid everything about her life growing up in poverty. She took modeling and etiquette classes, enrolled in college courses and became obsessed with marrying another wealthy man. After dating numerous high-profile jet setters, she met Johannes. He had recently graduated from Harvard Law School and took a year's vacation traveling throughout Europe. After about six months, he found himself ready to return to Ethiopia.

For Johannes, it was hard to turn down this woman who made herself easily available to him. He told her he didn't love her and had no intention of marrying her. But she came after him again and again. He tolerated her advances but in the far recesses of his mind, he knew something was wrong with Celine. He knew she wanted him for his title and money, but something else about her left a bad taste in his mouth. He believed she was mentally ill.

Johannes broke off his sexual relationship with Celine because she had become increasingly obsessed with the other women he dated. None of his relationships ever worked out. He never knew Celine had secretly hired Ali to keep an eye on all of his romantic endeavors. Without Johannes knowledge, Celine had effectively broken up all of his relationships with the women he dated by threatening their lives with anonymous phone calls. Johannes never knew why his relationships always seemed to fizzle out.

Ali had taken Celine up on her offer to spy on Johannes for a large sum of money. He had lived a hard life in Somalia. Money was more important to Ali than anything else in the world. He had seen too many of his countrymen die of starvation. He knew the cycle well. First the bloating of the stomach then came the coma. Both were common sights to him as a child. He vowed when he grew up he would never go hungry again. He would do whatever it took to rise out of poverty. He secretly loathed the privileged class, especially those as frivolous as Celine. She would never know how he detested her throwing her money around on her stupid plots. He spied for the money, nothing else. He made it a habit to keep up the facade of high regard for her.

Celine walked over to the Italian glass coffee table and removed the top of a footed crystal cigarette dish. Ali pulled out a disposable lighter from his pocket and flicked it when he saw her lift a cigarette to her mouth. Celine gave Ali a sidelong glance through a thick veil of smoke and led the way to the sliding glass door leading to the terrace. Ali followed her outside in the shivering cold evening air chilling him right down to his bones. He leaned on the wrought-iron rail and watched her inhale the cigarette smoke deeply.

Ali knew all too well that Celine was bothered by what he had told her about Shana. He was surprised Celine hadn't responded in a fit of anger. The last time he told her about one of Johannes' women, she threw a glass vase at him, grazing his temple, leaving a permanent scar on his eyebrow. The last thing he wanted to do was make this madwoman angry, at least until he got the money she owed him for the spy job on Shana.

"We must think of a plan," Celine stated with a jealous look.

Ali coughed as Celine blew smoke into his face. He quickly came up with an idea. He wanted to go back inside.

"Why don't you give Shana a call, like the others?" Ali offered.

Celine smiled at Ali's suggestion.

Ali took her cigarette, which had burned down to the butt, out of her hand and extinguished it in a marble ashtray situated on the wrought iron patio table.

"It has worked many times before, but do you think it will work on this woman?"

“Why wouldn’t it work? Ali said. “There’s nothing extraordinary about her.”

Celine walked back into the living room and picked up her handbag lying on the sofa. She pulled out some bills from her wallet and tossed them to Ali. “Keep me informed of where they go and try to get her cell phone number.”

***

The following Monday morning after Shana arrived at work; Mr. Withers called her into his office. “Sit down, Ms. Zachary, I have something important to discuss with you.”

Shana sat down in a chair and crossed her legs, “What is it, Mr. Withers?”

“Ms Zachary, you have been promoted to Senior International Loan Officer. Your new position requires extensive travel. How would you feel about working overseas this year?”

Shana’s eyes widened when she heard the word overseas.

“We need to establish a field office in Nairobi, Kenya, to keep a close eye on how the countries in East Africa are handling the monetary funds the U.S. government has recently loaned them. You are being offered this opportunity because your background and experience make you the most likely candidate.”

He continued while twisting a pencil between his fingers. “Your salary will triple and your benefits will include paid housing, chefs and housekeepers. This assignment is not without risk. We have received many communications about fighting in East Africa.” He paused. “Ms. Zachary, are you listening?”

Shana stopped listening after she heard the word “overseas.” She’d always dreamed of working abroad, and this was the chance of a lifetime. She’d worked hard for this promotion, and it finally came through.

“Well, what do you think?” Mr. Withers asked.

“I...I don’t know what to say.” Shana sat with a blank stare on her face. I’ve dreamed of this day since I was a child.”

“I’ll take that for a yes.”

“Yes...Mr. Withers. I would be honored to serve in Nairobi.”

“So let’s get down to the details.” Mr. Withers urged. “When you arrive in Nairobi, you will meet with Dr. Burnham. He’s a retired Lieutenant in the British military. He will brief you on current affairs, culture, economics, and the politics of East Africa. He will also provide you with security. Your mission is to establish a field office four our agency in the same building as the American Embassy. You will report directly to me in the initial stages by sending a monthly status report with an analysis of all loan prospects, outstanding loans, and an update on the political situation. A lot of development is going on in Africa now. We want to start working on this project as soon as possible. Can you be ready to travel within thirty days?"

Shana was in a daze. She still couldn't believe her ears. When she returned to reality, she realized Mr. Withers was waiting for her answer. "What was the question again?"

"Can you be ready to travel within thirty days?"

Shana regained her thoughts and replied. "Yes, Mr. Withers. I can be ready in thirty days." Her next thought was of Johannes. How was she going to tell him?

"Good, your plane tickets will be paid for in advance, and I will personally escort you to the airport on the day of your departure."

Shana sat thinking about how she could lease her townhouse, pack her bags and be ready to go within thirty days. After she left his office, she immediately called her aunt and started making arrangements to lease her property.

To avoid thinking about how she was going to tell Johannes, she busied herself until it was time to leave for the day.

Five o'clock came quickly. Shana went straight home through the heavy traffic with Johannes on her mind.

Once she arrived at her house, she kicked off her shoes and drew a bubble bath. A moment later her cell phone rang. It was Johannes. She cautiously answered the call.

"Hello, beautiful. How did your day go?"

She paused for a second. "My day went fine. I'm still recuperating from our weekend." Not yet sure how she would break the news to Johannes, she hardly heard any of his conversation.

"Shana?" Johannes asked.

"Yes," she muttered uneasily. "I…, I have a lot on my mind. I have something to tell..."

Johannes interrupted her. "Are we still on for tonight?"

"Of course," she said biting her lip looking around the room.

"Then I will pick you up at seven thirty."

"Okay, but I need to talk to you about something this evening."

"You can talk to me when I pick you up. I worked hard all day, and I look forward to seeing you tonight."

"Okay Johannes, I'll see you tonight."

When Johannes arrived, he pushed the button to ring her doorbell. Shana came out dressed in a pair of salmon linen slacks and a matching blouse. "How was your day?" she said kissing him on the cheek, avoiding eye contact.

Johannes sensed something was wrong because she appeared distracted.

"Here. Let me take your coat," Shana said nervously taking his coat and hanging it on the coat rack. She led him into the living room.

Johannes remained standing until she sat. He wondered what had happened since yesterday to make her act so distant. What did she have to tell him?

Shana crossed her legs at the ankle and nervously patted the soft cushion next to her. "I have something to tell you, Johannes."

Johannes sat. "What is on your mind, My Dove?" Johannes asked.

Bracing herself, Shana looked directly into his eyes and took a deep breath. "I was offered an assignment today to work in Nairobi, Kenya." She quickly exhaled.

Johannes' heart sank as he listened to her. He stared at her for a long moment. All sorts of thoughts ran through his mind. His jaw twitched with a twinge of disappointment. Why would she want to take a job overseas, now their relationship was beginning to blossom? His mind recalled the steamy scene on her front porch yesterday when she told him she would be his girlfriend. "Well what are you going to do?" he asked.

Shana lowered her eyes. "I am going to accept." She looked up and noticed the wrinkles forming on his forehead.

"Shana, I can't lie…I will miss you terribly. He cheered up when he thought about it. "Nairobi is not far from Ethiopia. I can come to visit you because I'll be returning to Ethiopia shortly." Johannes said confidently. "We will be apart for a short time."

"Thank you for being understanding Johannes. I've always dreamed of working overseas."

Johannes put his index finger to her lips and pulled her closer to him, whispering into her ear. "Let's make the best of the time we have left."

Shana smiled, feeling reassured by his words.

He slipped his arms around her waist and brushed his face against her slender copper neck, releasing her sensual woodsy fragrance. Shana melted like butter in his hands, and then moaned as she fell under his spell. She remembered how good it felt to be held in his strong arms. She could feel the rippling muscles of his arms through his shirt.

Panting and breathless, she closed her eyes as his searching lips found hers. His hands wandered down her back and caressed her spine, all the time pressing her body closer to his. He could feel the ample curve of her hips and breasts as he moved his hands over the softness of her blouse. Passion raged like a burning fire within his body, as he covered her lips and neck with his burning kisses. He whispered softly into her ear, "Shana, you do not know the powers you possess over me."

Johannes had indeed fallen in love with Shana. She was the woman who could make him change his inflexible, uncompromising ways. If she'd been any other woman, he would have demanded she stay. He wanted to make love to her right now, but he decided to wait until Shana was ready for lovemaking. He'd wait an eternity, for Shana. She was everything he wanted in a woman.

"So when do you leave?" Johannes asked as he kissed the palm of her hand.

Shana sat up straight. "In thirty days."

"Where will you be working?" Johannes questioned.

Shana held his hand and murmured, "The U.S. Embassy in downtown Nairobi."

Johannes knew exactly where it was. He'd been to the Embassy many times. He knew the British officer in charge of the U.S. Embassy in Nairobi.

He also knew the president of Kenya on a first name basis. He would arrange for Shana to be well protected and looked after, without her ever knowing. He owned a beach house in Mombasa on the coast of Kenya, which was an eight-hour drive from Nairobi. He made a mental note to take Shana to the house and spend some time together. It was not a problem for Shana to live and work in Nairobi. If all went well with the amendments, he would be in Ethiopia within the next two months, and Shana would be eight hours away. He smiled.

"I will take you to the airport when it's time for you to leave."

"Mr. Withers wants to escort me to the airport. He's like a father to me."

Johannes paused at Shana's statement. He was unaccustomed to women telling him what he could not do. He changed the conversation around to discuss how he felt about her. "There is something I want to give you, Shana." He pulled out a brilliant emerald ring from his pocket and placed it on her finger. He truly believed Shana would be his future wife. "I want you to keep this. It once belonged to my mother. It is supposed to bring good luck." He smiled and looked deeply into her eyes. "It will one day bring us back together."

"Johannes, I...can't accept this." She shook her head, refusing him.

Johannes wouldn't take no for an answer. He

believed he and Shana would end up together. No ocean, sea, mountain or valley could keep him away from the woman he loved.

"Will you join me for dinner at my place on Friday?" Johannes asked.

Shana nodded her head in the affirmative.

"I will have Ababa prepare a scrumptious Ethiopian meal I am sure you will enjoy."

Chapter 12

Ali drove past the security guards at the gate and up the circular driveway to Johannes estate. Shana saw him standing on the front porch waiting for her. Once Ali stopped the car, Johannes walked up and opened the back door.

"Every time I see you, you look even more beautiful than the last." His eyes scanned her figure.

Shana stepped out of the limousine wearing an elegant, winter-white dinner suit, accessorized with pearls. She smiled at his compliment.

Johannes pulled her into his embrace. Shana buried her face against the corded muscles of his chest. His mouth covered her hungrily in a seductive kiss. He didn't care who saw them. He raised his mouth from hers, gazing into her eyes and said, "I have missed you, My Dove."

"I missed you too," she said shocked at her eager response to his kiss.

He took her by the hand, and walked with her inside the house. "Are you hungry?"

"I'm starving."

They walked into the dining room to a table set for a king. Johannes pulled out a chair for Shana. "I have something important I want to ask you tonight." He pushed her chair. "But first, we'll have a traditional Ethiopian dinner Ababa has prepared."

"Sounds great Johannes," Shana said taking a sip of water.

Ababa brought out a plate of injera bread, some braised beef with carrots and potatoes and a tossed green salad, and a plate of warm towels.

Shana saw a small bowl filled with lemon water next to her plate. She looked for the silverware but saw none.

Johannes observed her looking for the utensils. "In Ethiopia, we eat with our fingers." He dipped his fingers into the bowl of lemon water and dried them with a warm towel. Shana followed suit.

Johannes tore a small piece of the flat bread. "This is called injera."

Shana took a small piece and tasted it. "It's good."

Johannes scooped some beef and vegetables from the large bowl onto Shana's plate, then his. "You dip a piece of bread into the beef like this," he said placing a small piece of bread over the meat. "Then you scoop it up and eat it."

Shana followed Johannes example. "Mmm, this is good."

Johannes poured Shana some wine from a carafe. "This is called Honey Wine."

Shana's face lit up after taking a sip. "This is good. It's sweet like honey."

"Some call it Nectar of the Gods," Johannes said smiling.

"I know of an Ethiopian restaurant in San Francisco. I've always wanted to eat at the restaurant, but I never had the chance. Now I see what I've been missing."

They both enjoyed their meal and drinking their honey wine well into the evening. After dinner, they went into what Johannes called the blue room. They sat on a pale blue sofa in front of the fireplace.

Johannes took Shana's hand into his and saw she was wearing his mother's emerald ring. "I have a question for you Shana."

"What?" Shana said looking into his eyes.

"Can you imagine yourself being married to me?"

Shana was too surprised to open her mouth. She was at a complete loss for words.

Johannes noticed his question had caught her off guard.

"Don't you think it is a little too early to ask me that question?"

"Shana, I love you. I have no doubt in my mind—I want you to be my wife."

"Are you asking me to marry you?"

"In a way, yes. But first I want you to think about how your life would change."

"How would it change?"

"For one thing, you would have to give up your career."

"Give up my career? I've worked too hard to get my promotion to give it up to get married. Why would I have to give up my career? Don't they have working women in Ethiopia?"

"Yes, we have working royals, but your public role as my wife would come before your private role as a career woman. You would be required to make official appearances with me to the world.

Shana's voice began to shake. "I..., I would have to give up my career?" She tried to regain her composure. "What about my private life?"

"Your privacy would end as you know it. You would have security following you around everywhere," he said. "But at a discreet distance," he added. He gave her an inquisitive look.

"Haven't you noticed my security following us around?"

"Yes. I have."

"Do you think you could ever live that way?"

"I don't know Johannes."

"You would get used to it."

"What if I am not accepted? I am after all, an American."

"You are not the first American to marry a royal. Princess Grace was an American, who married Prince Rainier of Monaco. She gave up her Hollywood career after their marriage. My people would accept you because I accept you."

"So how else would my life change?"

"Well, you would have to move to my family's residence in Addis Ababa. Your itinerary might include attending a formal dinner or two on a consistent basis, traveling with me internationally, and presiding over a full household staff for a large estate."

"I don't know if I could live a royal lifestyle for the rest of my life Johannes. Why don't we slow down? I need more time to think."

"I want you to get a glimpse of how your life would change." Johannes felt relieved he'd told her.

"Can't you compromise on my privacy? Don' any flexibility with your security?"

I'm sorry Shana, but I cannot compromise on this way of life."

"You have the power to do whatever you want. I believe you can compromise. When I asked you about your flaws, you told me you had a tendency to be inflexible. You also told me you didn't like to be controlled. I wonder if your lack of compromise is more about your problem with control."

"I told you I am not a control freak!" Johannes frowned. He knew how important Shana's career was to her, but she needed to understand his position. Since she didn't give back his ring, he assumed she seriously considered his proposal. He changed the conversation to her job in Nairobi because he didn't want to press his luck.

Ali overheard their conversation as he walked by a guard who knew him on a first-name basis. He slipped into the library when he heard Shana and Johannes involved in a serious conversation. He saw Johannes cell phone on his desk. He turned on the phone but saw it required a password. He walked around Johannes desk looking for Shana's number jotted down somewhere. Finally, he saw it scribbled on a post-it note. He wrote down the number, stuffed it into his pants pocket and walked out as casually as he'd walked in.

Late in the evening, Shana lay in her bed thinking of her conversation with Johannes. He gave her a lot to think about with his question. She appreciated him explaining how her life would change if she married him. But her life was about to change after she moved to Nairobi. She imagined she would go through some culture shock with the people and the language, although she spoke Swahili. Maybe working and living in Kenya, would prepare her for life with Johannes in Ethiopia, she thought. She'd always heard love conquers all. She knew she loved Johannes, but she didn't like his rigid attitude and didn't look forward to losing her private life. She valued her privacy and loved her career and didn't want to give up either one. She pulled the covers over her head and went to sleep.

At three o'clock in the morning, Shana's cell phone woke her up from a deep sleep. "What!" She sat up in the bed. Something must be wrong, she thought. She hoped it wasn't her aunt. She looked at the display window and saw the call was from an unknown number.

"Hello," she said answering the call.

"Leave Johannes alone or die." Celine pressed the pound key several times before ending the call.

"What? Who is this?" Shana sat up in the bed. "Some nut," she thought. Then she remembered hearing Johannes name.

Her phone rang again. Shana saw it was from the same number. She answered the call and the same thing happened.

Celine had called Shana with threats all night long after the first call. Shana finally turned off her phone after Celine told her she was pregnant by Johannes."

Startled and confused, Shana decided to wait until she had a chance to ask Johannes if he knew a woman who spoke with a slight French accent. Shana's emotions overtook her logic before she went back to sleep. Who was this man she thought she loved?

First thing in the morning, Shana called Johannes. Before he could greet her, she said, "a woman with a French accent called me all night long threatening to kill me. She claims to be pregnant by you."

"Celine!" Johannes growled.

Celine's image came to his mind. She was at it again, he thought. Celine thought Johannes didn't know she had been sabotaging his relationships for years. After a third relationship had fizzled out, he had his ex-girlfriend Celine investigated. He found out she had threatened all of his ex-girlfriends. He could have easily had her arrested, but couldn't because he knew Celine suffered from emotional problems. He had talked to her several times telling her to get some help. He was honest and told her he was not going to marry her. She ignored Johannes' rejection. It was obvious she had no intention to stop harassing his romantic interests. Johannes thought he might have to have her arrested.

"Is Celine her name?" Shana asked.

"She's crazy Shana. She is not pregnant by me."

"So how do you know this woman?"

"I dated her several years ago. She has emotional problems."

"So what are you going to do about her?"

Johannes paused for a moment. "I'll stop the calls."

How many women like her did Johannes have in his life? Shana wondered. "I didn't think you were involved with another woman, especially after you asked me to be your girlfriend?" Shana was completely disappointed. "I love you Johannes, but right now I see too many red lights flashing to think of marrying you."

"What do you mean too many red lights?"

"First, I would have to end my career. Second, I would have to lose my privacy. Third, I would have to deal with this crazy woman's threats. How many women like her are in your life, Johannes? I never asked you before, especially after you asked me to marry you."

Johannes remained silent after hearing her say she would not marry him.

At this point, Shana decided to pull back. "Johannes, I told you I would think about your proposal and I have. I've decided I cannot marry you. I will give your mother's ring back."

"Shana, please don't do this."

"I'm sorry Johannes." She ended the call.

Johannes called her right back, but she'd turned off her phone. He got dressed and drove to her place, but her car was gone. He rang her doorbell, but she didn't answer. He took out a memo pad and pen and wrote Shana a note. "Please Shana, I need to talk to you. Things are not as they seem. Please call me, I will be waiting for your call. Johannes"

What Johannes didn't know was Shana was at Lauren's house spilling her heart out about Celine and having to give up her career. Lauren lent a sympathetic ear to her friend.

Several days passed by, and Johannes could not get in touch with Shana. She ignored all of his attempts to contact her. On the third day, he waited outside her job in San Francisco. When she walked through the door, he stopped her. "Shana." He said to get her attention.

She turned around and saw him leaning against the building. He began walking with her down the street. "Please stop and talk to me, Shana."

Shana stopped.

"Ali is parked across the street. Can I talk to you in the limousine?"

"Fine." Shana thought this would be a good time to give him his mother's ring.

When they reached the limousine, Johannes told Ali to take a break, pointing to a coffee shop across the street. He opened the back door for Shana. "Shana, please forgive me for not handling Celine in a more effective way."

Shana took the emerald ring off of her finger and handed it to Johannes. "Celine is the easy part of this problem. I don't want to give up my privacy to live a life of a princess. I know most women, like Celine would give up everything at the chance of marrying you, but not me."

"What if you had no public duties for the first two years?"

"I don't have a problem with the public duties. I have a problem with losing my privacy and my career. I'm sorry Johannes." She handed the ring to Johannes.

Johannes put his mother's ring in the palm of

her hand and curled it up. "Keep it for now. It will bring us back together."

Shana opened the door and got out of the car, leaving Johannes in the backseat.

***

One day on her way to lunch, Shana looked through her wallet to check to see how much cash she had. She fumbled through a twenty dollar bill and two fives. Then she came across the ticket stubs from the ballet. Tears began to trickle down her face as she remembered that eventful day. Every night she lay in bed crying herself to sleep. The revelation came to her one night. She should have listened to her gut feeling, which told her never to trust herself with love.

Another week had passed. Johannes knew Shana would be leaving for Kenya in a couple of days. He parked his car outside her house one day until she came home. He saw her drive up and get out of his car. "Shana, please I must speak with you."

Shana hurried past him.

He grabbed her arm and gave her a serious look. "Shana please."

"Johannes stop. I'm not going to change my mind."

Chapter 13

The San Francisco International Airport was cold and crowded with passengers meeting relatives visiting for the upcoming holidays. Shana stood at the Kenya Airways terminal with Mr. Withers, who gave the gate agent the last of her bags.

"Well, Ms. Zachary, your big day is finally here. Good luck with your new assignment," Mr. Withers said as he handed Shana her carry-on luggage.

"Thanks, Mr. Withers," Shana said, holding her hand out.

Mr. Withers pulled Shana to himself and gave her a fatherly hug. "I'm sure everything will work out fine. You are a strong, intelligent woman, and I have a lot of confidence in you."

"I promise, Mr. Withers, I will do a good job, I'll make you proud of me," Shana said. Her hazel-bronze eyes watered as she released herself from Mr. Withers bear hug. She stepped onto the escalator waving good-bye as she ascended skyward. When she reached the second floor, she and saw Mr. Withers pull out a white cotton handkerchief to wipe his eyes.

After she stepped off the escalator, she walked toward the Kenya Airways security area. She was surprised to see the line crowded with people wearing long, flowing robes in every color under the sun, all in sharp contrast to the people standing in the other airline security lines.

The air crackled with excitement as Shana walked toward the roped area and took her place in line. She didn't mind the long wait. She was quite content observing the activities going on around her. She noticed some of the women had braided their hair into tiny little braids and then restyled them into French rolls, ponytails, and bobs. Some of them wore tailored dresses with African prints, and others wore traditional African gowns.

A man and a woman, both dressed in flowing gowns, stood in front of Shana ready to check in several large cardboard boxes. Shana asked the man what they had purchased. He said with a thick British accent, "Why, bed linens. They're three times the cost in Kenya."

After Shana passed through security, she decided to hunt down a store that sold cold bottled water. "Finally," she sighed. She saw a little store on the other side of the generic ATM. She walked in and saw a huge selection of magazines displayed on a wall shelf. She chose a Travel and Leisure magazine with a photo of The Sphinx on the cover.

On the far end of the shelf was a copy of Africa Today. A full-blown picture of the city of Gondar, Ethiopia was on the cover with a caption, "Can there be peace in Ethiopia?" Shana never saw the magazine. She purchased her magazine and a bottle of water and then walked over to her departure gate.

Since Shana had to wait thirty minutes, she read the article about the history of the Sphinx. Her excitement made her mind hard for her to concentrate. When she finally boarded the plane, she was pleasantly surprised to see African prints echoed in the drapery and upholstery. Posters and advertisements painted with headhunter artwork and other African motifs also decorated the interior. Flight attendants walked down the aisle wearing dashiki's and slacks or and colorful printed dresses.

Once the plane took off, Shana looked down at the earth and thought about Johannes. She asked herself if pursuing her career was more important than living a life married to Johannes. Her heart ached with conflicting emotions. She gathered her composure and refused to answer the question.

A woman with a thick African accent spoke over the loud speaker interrupting Shana's thoughts. She recited the air flight safety message, and then announced a long layover in Amsterdam. She repeated the message in Swahili and English.

Shana made friends with the young woman sitting next to her. She found out the woman was a student at the University of California, returning home to visit her parents in Nairobi. Shana chatted with her until she fell asleep.

It was eight in the morning when the plane

made the first layover in Amsterdam. The plane landed smoothly, and all of the passengers clapped in unison, giving the pilot a round of applause. Shana was shocked when she saw a young black man step from behind the cockpit. She felt slightly nervous because she had never been on a plane flown by a black pilot.

A female flight attendant announced over the speaker. "We will have an eighteen-hour layover. Anyone wishing to disembark can leave as long you are back on time."

Shana decided to get off and walk around the terminal for a while. She signed up for a five hour tour of Amsterdam. When she returned, she fell asleep in a comfortable chair until her flight was ready to board for Nairobi.

Chapter 14

The smoldering heat engulfed Shana as soon as she stepped off the plane. The time was two in the afternoon when the plane arrived in Nairobi. A tall, thin blonde haired man with a thick mustache, and watery gray eyes stood at the gate entrance. He watched intensely through wire-rimmed spectacles at all of the people disembarking from the plane. Hot from wearing a white summer suit and a light blue shirt and tie, he used a damp white handkerchief to wipe perspiration from his face. He was holding a sign with her name.

The man approached Shana and spoke with a heavy British Accent. “Are you Shana Zachary?”

Shana scanned him up and down and asked to see his identification. He showed her his British Passport. Shana looked at his picture and read his name. He was Dr. Clifford D. Burnham, British Diplomat. He was indeed the official from the American Embassy, who was supposed to meet her at the airport. She nodded her head. “Yes, I am Shana Zachary.”

“How was your flight, Miss?” he said while taking her carryon bags. He knew from his contact with Mr. Withers, that Shana was a young African American female, but he hadn’t expected her to look this beautiful.

"The flight was long, but I'm fine." Shana followed Dr. Burnham into the airport where they waited for her luggage. Shana pulled her bags off of the carousel. A small man quickly took her luggage from her hands. He took her carryon bags in a rough manner and put them with the other luggage on a cart. Once outside he put them all in the trunk of Dr. Burnham's black Mercedes sedan.

"Take your time with those bags, Maji," Dr. Burnham commanded. Shortly after that, he introduced the small man with a receding hairline to Shana.

"This is Maji, he will be your driver and guide."

Shana asked him to repeat his name.

"Ma-jee," he said several times with a grin on his face. Once inside the car, Shana asked "Dr. Burnham. Where are we going?"

"We are going to your new residence."

Shana sighed with relief. She wanted to lie down and get some rest.

After leaving the airport, Maji drove down a long dirt road densely lined with banana trees and other tropical foliage. After about fifteen minutes, they approached a white two-story Mediterranean-style structure made of wood and stucco. Exotic trees and flowers surrounded the building. She saw the edge of a swimming pool in the back. A straw umbrella attached to a tabletop surrounded by four rattan chairs were situated on the verandah. A temporary burst of energy came over Shana, as she saw her new home.

Maji opened the car door and a small-framed woman met them with a warm smile and cool drinks served inside coconut hulls. Maji introduced the petite woman as his wife. “This is my wife, Layla.”

Shana smiled and introduced herself. “My name is Shana.”

“You arrived in time,” Layla said in perfect English. “I have prepared one of my favorite dishes I think you all will enjoy. I hope you are hungry.”

Shana replied, “Yes, I am Layla, but I’m also exhausted from my flight.”

Layla smiled as she handed Shana a napkin for her drink. “Maji will take your bags to your room. Come, follow me, you and Dr. Burnham can wash your hands and prepare for a meal.”

After Shana and Dr. Burnham refreshed themselves, they came into the dining room.

“Everything looks delicious Layla, like a page out of a magazine,” Shana remarked.

Layla blushed and smiled at the compliment. “I try to keep the place spotless.”

After Shana and Dr. Burnham had finished their meal of grilled fish, green salad, and chilled mangoes for dessert, they sat and talked a while, then decided to take a short tour of the premises.

The drawing room, adjacent to the dining room was filled with elegant Masai sculpture along with carved masks and ivory artifacts. An exotic butterfly collection hung tastefully on a wall in the library. Zebra and leopard skins covered the polyurethane hardwood floors in the drawing room and library. A dramatic staircase made of ebony hardwood separated the upper east and west wings of the house. African fabrics in red, black, blue, and gold echoed in the upholstery and drapery everywhere. Shana had never seen a house like this before. She loved the open, airy feeling of the architecture. Everywhere she looked she saw open windows, allowing the cool breeze to flow through.

They walked outside around the back and saw Maji, who joined them on the tour. He showed them a miniature waterfall, pouring into a swimming pool conveniently located near the kitchen. Lush, pink and red hibiscus flowers dominated the garden and surrounded the green freshly cut lawn. Shana was impressed.

After the tour, Shana excused herself, informing Dr. Burnham she was tired. Dr. Burnham told Shana he would pick her up and take her to the American Embassy, first thing Monday morning.

Layla led Shana to her bedroom. "This is the

master bedroom," she said proudly.

Shana looked around the large white room and noticed a large ceiling fan above the queen size bed. A mosquito net draped over the bed covered in white linens. She saw a dressing room through an arched doorway. She peeked into the dressing room and saw a large wardrobe closet and a dressing table. She walked back into the bedroom and walked through a sliding glass door leading onto a private verandah with a table and chairs. She leaned on the bamboo railing and looked into a vista revealing a tropical landscape filled with flowers and shrubs, unlike anything she'd ever seen. The Garden of Eden couldn't have looked more beautiful, she whispered to herself. She closed her eyes and listened to the sounds of parrots calling each other. She inhaled the fresh sweet air and stopped to think of her blessings. In the middle of the afternoon, she felt compelled to get into bed. She pulled back the mosquito net and slid into bed fully clothed. The last thing she saw was the ceiling fan slowly turning.

For the next two days, Shana woke up early and ate a light continental breakfast of chilled fruit, toast, and coffee.

***

By the time Monday morning came, Dr. Burnham arrived early to pick up Shana for her first day on the job. He knocked on her door after adjusting his trousers and spectacles. He was pleasantly surprised to see how attractive she looked wearing a white sleeveless dress when she opened the door. "I see you are up bright and early. Are you ready for your first day on the job?"

"I'm excited," Shana said closing the door.

The U. S. Embassy came into sight as Maji drove down Harambee Avenue. The modern two-story building was located in the southwest corner of downtown next to the American Culture Center and cattycorner to the Kenyatta Conference Center. The embassy constructed with open windows running the entire length of the building, had an old-world continental charm. She remembered discussing with Mr. Withers that the Embassy was subject to a completely different set of international standards and laws.

Two armed U.S. military guards stood in front of the building when Mr. Burnham and Shana arrived. When they walked into the embassy, they were greeted by two women and two young men.

Dr. Burnham introduced Shana to the staff. "Lisa will be your secretary," he stated. Both of the women were descendants of settlers who stayed in Nairobi after Kenya won independence from Britain. The two young men were Kikuyu. Dr. Burnham explained to the staff that Shana was their new manager.

"We will all be your interpreters. If you have any questions or need anything at all simply ask any one of us. By the way, I forgot to mention, I made reservations for dinner tonight at the Nairobi Safari Club. Is six okay?"

"Six is fine," Shana said nodding in agreement.

"Come, let's go into the conference room. I have some financial reports I want to show you."

Shana followed Dr. Burnham. They stayed in the conference room most of the morning. Before lunch, he gave her a tour of the embassy and showed Shana to her new office. Shana stayed in her office for a while to get used to her surroundings. She closed her eyes for a moment, to meditate and give thanks for this wonderful experience. She ran her hand along the teak executive desk and credenza admiring the sleek design. Someone had placed her briefcase by the door. She laid the briefcase on her desk, and began removing paperwork.

After thirty minutes of organizing her workspace, Shana heard a knock on her door. Dr. Burnham stuck his head inside. "It's time for lunch. We can go to a small restaurant down the road."

Shana interrupted. "No, Dr. Burnham, I'm not very hungry. I don't usually eat lunch."

"Well come with me to get some fresh air," Dr. Burnham said with a smile on his face. They stopped at a little restaurant on the outskirts of town and ordered roasted chicken and rice which Shana could not eat because she had no appetite.

When they returned to the office from lunch, the rest of the afternoon went by quickly. They left the office at four thirty. When Shana arrived home, she took a bath and ate dinner by herself.

For the next several weeks, Shana's daily activities were uneventful. Some parts of her job were boring, but she always enjoyed meeting new members of the business community. She loved having the freedom to recommend loans to whomever she found qualified. She particularly enjoyed consulting with her business colleagues about making necessary adjustments in their practices to bring about greater profits.

For the next two months, Shana developed a routine to keep herself busy. She woke up in the morning, went to work for eight hours, met with clients, and came back home to spend her evenings relaxing on the verandah. On Friday nights, like back home, she went to the movies. She was slightly fearful of venturing out on her own at night. Most of the time, she stuck close to home. Sometimes Layla would talk with her at night about her relatives and tell her stories. She was comfortable with the routine at first, but then one night Layla repeated the same story twice. Shana realized she was lonely. She missed Johannes.

As the days passed, a gnawing feeling settled in the pit of Shana's stomach forewarning her she was following in her Aunt's footsteps. All of her loneliness and confusion welded together in one upsurge of devouring yearning, she still loved Johannes. One night, she dreamt she was old, frail, and alone. She woke up from her nightmare in a cold sweat. She realized she had made the mistake of a lifetime by choosing her career over Johannes. She regretted her choice. She flung herself from her bed and walked over to the window. She could hear the whisper of his voice in the warm breeze. Staring into the darkness, she set her eyes on the moon and the stars.

The longer she gazed at the shining celestial body, the more she thought about Johannes. He's such a kind, loving, patient man, she pondered. He poured out his feelings to her and even now touched her heart with the memory of his ways. She remembered how he'd melted the wall of ice surrounding her heart until her fear of intimacy faded away. Since time had passed, she was now in touch with her feelings. She found herself yearning to feel his touch, his kiss, and his strong embrace. She wiped away hot tears with the back of her hands as they rolled down her cheeks. For the first time in her life, she understood the value of love.

***

Johannes sighed as he stared into the darkness out of the airplane window. Two months had passed since Shana left, and he missed her terribly. He had finally finished the amendments to the constitution earlier in the week and was on his way home to present the new document to Parliament for a vote and the United Nations. As he looked through the window, he saw Shana's face in the stars. She is a woman of many contradictions, he thought. She is full of life yet afraid to live. Frightened of love, yet her passionate kisses still burn in my heart. She is unlike any woman I have ever known. I forget my troubles when I am around her. I constantly imagine making love with her. His mind turned toward lustful thoughts. He rubbed his aching forehead from the memories. I cannot stop loving her, he thought to himself. I have to get her back.

Chapter 15

When Ali pulled up to the family estate, Johannes saw his father sitting on the terrace in his wheelchair. Johannes went upstairs and greeted his father with a wide embrace.

Tears of joy flowed down his father's face as he saw his son return home. "My son, did you finish the amendments?"

"I finished, father," Johannes said giving his father a serious look. "But first things first," he said looking at his father. "How are you feeling, father?" He noticed his father's coloring had turned a dull gray.

"I feel fine, my son."

Johannes turned his father's wheelchair around and rolled him back inside. "You need to lie down. You do not look well." Johannes helped him back into bed. He watched him lean back and exhale. The tension seemed to melt from his father's face now the document had been completed. After catching up on family matters, Johannes kissed his father on the forehead and left the room.

He immediately went to his office and had Rebecca call the Council members for a meeting. Meanwhile, Bari walked into Johannes' office. Johannes had called Bari earlier to discuss presenting the new constitution to Parliament for a vote and the UN.

Bari embraced Johannes. “Welcome home, Johannes.”

Johannes returned his embrace. “I’m glad to be home, my friend.

Suddenly Rebecca came in with a breaking news report. Johannes read the document and froze.

“What?” Bari said.

“It’s Warlord Kefa and his army. They have attacked a small border town killing innocent women and children.”

“Kefa!” Bari growled under his voice.

General Matobe, Johannes’ military advisor walked in greeting him. “Your Grace, I see by the look on your face you’ve heard the bad news. We all knew Kefa has been building up his army and planning a military coup.”

Johannes stomached churned.

“Your Grace, you and your family should leave the country for a while,” Matobe advised with a concerned look on his face. He continued to speak but was abruptly halted.

“No!” Johannes shouted as he pounded his fist on his desk. “I will never let that renegade run me out of my country." Johannes barked. "There is one way to stop his army. Now is the time to introduce the amendments to Parliament and the United Nations. Most of Kefa's men are the very ones our political system has excluded for centuries. Once they understand the new constitution will guarantee equal rights to every single Ethiopian without regard to his or her ethnicity, they will see the futility of being part of Kefa's army."

Bari leaned back in his chair and crossed his legs. "When do you plan on presenting the document?"

"Next week."

***

The long motorcade of Mercedes limousines and sedans drove through the intolerable midday heat toward the border town of Djibouti near the Red Sea. General Motabe held his hand up to block a flash of bright light coming from a mountain about a mile away. He had come to invite some local leaders to the United Nations to discuss the new constitution he hoped would end the fighting.

He looked out and saw the flashing light again and asked his driver if he had seen the flash. Before his driver could reply, General Motabe looked beyond the horizon and saw a group of green Jeeps advancing in the distance. A whirlwind of dirt flew behind a man standing in the passenger's seat of a jeep, holding a rifle under his arm aiming to fire at the motorcade. "It's that jackal Kefa Dalmar," General Motabe growled. Then he saw more jeeps coming with armed men standing in the passenger's seat. "We're under attack!" Motabe yelled out.

General Matobe's men quickly relied on their UN peacekeeping training. All drivers parked their vehicles closely together and formed an arc. They all opened their doors as shields to ward off the anticipated firefight. Motabe did what he normally did in situations like this—he pulled out his firearm, rolled out of his vehicle, and hit the dirt. His men never had to worry about themselves or the General during a firefight, because they had been trained to handle all kinds of contingency situations.

Gunshots could be heard from miles around. The General looked up and saw they were outnumbered five to one, which did not intimidate him. He turned to his left and saw a man standing in a Jeep about one hundred yards away waving his arms around like a madman, giving instructions to the other renegades. He aimed right at the renegade's forehead and pulled the trigger and watched him fall out of the jeep. Then he aimed and hit the driver and saw the Jeep spin out of control, slamming into another vehicle. Suddenly he felt a burning sensation on the side of his head and realized he had been grazed with a minor flesh wound. He continued to fire until another seven went down.

The General could hear the men yelling their war cries as the firing went on. After ten minutes of fierce fighting, between the two groups, he saw two jeeps retreat, one heaped with dead bodies and the other with wounded. After the dust had settled and the renegades retreated, Motabe wiped the sweat from his brow and got back into his vehicle, commanding everyone in the motorcade to return home.

***

After General Motabe returned, he cleaned himself up and went to see Johannes to give his after action report.

Johannes gave General Motabe a withering stare when he saw the bandage on the side of the general's face.

General Motabe offered an explanation. "Warlord Kefa Dalmar and his thugs are patrolling the border towns."

Johannes' eyes were as hard as granite. "I know his tactics well. He doesn't want peace or the new constitution. He and his bloodthirsty jackals have caused havoc since the civil war began." Johannes said rubbing his shoulder.

"I agree, Dalmar does not want peace. He is a power seeking man who intimidates and controls the people in the border towns with his bloodthirsty army," Motabe said. "He saw our motorcade as a threat to his control and attacked. I am determined to prevent his surprise attacks from happening again. We will be ready for him the next time." General Motabe asserted.

Johannes paced the floor. His tone was relatively civil in spite of his anger. "If Dalmar thinks his attacks will prevent me from presenting the constitution to Parliament and the United Nations, he has another thing coming. His attacks make me more determined. Next week, I plan to invite leaders from every major ethnic groups to the UN and introduce the new constitution."

***

The majestic green, yellow and red flag whipped in the wind from the antenna of Johannes' limousine, which was the first of a long procession of leaders and their security. They all lined the street leading to the United Nations building. As each limousine reached the UN entrance, a chauffeur came around to open the door for the leader.

"Splendor of God," Johannes uttered as he watched the event through the window of the United Nations chapel, where he had been in prayer all morning. "It is time."

Armed security escorted each leader to the reception room where they were served food and drink. UN guards were positioned at each entrance of the building.

Johannes motioned Nadir to come and help him

tie his red sash around his uniform, which had come loose. He needed to hurry since the meeting would start promptly at ten o'clock. He squared his shoulders before exiting the doors of the chapel and descended the stairs in regal splendor.

Minutes later Johannes leaned back on his heels near the alcove in the meeting room. Bari and several key members of the powerful Council of Representatives took seats at the head table on the dais. Each leader and his entourage were seated in chairs in the audience.

Johannes had a serious look on his face—his mouth was clearly defined. He kept his lips firmly pressed together to maintain a powerful image. In full uniform, Johannes looked tall, regal, and solidly built. Although his fingers were long, his palms were strong and square in shape.

Johannes looked around the room, silently observing each leader as they skeptically observed him. Although he detested crowds immensely, he knew this one act was for the good of his country. He felt confident, focused, and proud of himself for getting all of the major leaders together under one roof. Thoughts of his ancient ancestor, Menelik I crossed his mind. He must have felt like this when the surrounding tribes accepted his leadership centuries ago, Johannes thought.

Each leader wore similar clothing but spoke a different dialect. Johannes knew most of the leaders by name and face; some hated him and some loved him. He was shocked to see Kefa Dalmar, actually showed up. Johannes balled his hands into fists when thought about how Dalmar had caused the deaths of many innocent people. Johannes had informed the head of the UN security to keep an alert eye on Dalmar if he showed his face.

Johannes observed the leaders whispering into the ears of each other. He hushed the conversations and opened up the meeting. Translators interpreted Johannes speech to everyone through headphones.

"Greetings. I have called this meeting today for several reasons. Our country is in the midst of a civil war. Our diverse ethnic groups have been fighting for centuries. Today I want to introduce these amendments to guarantee equality for every Ethiopian, regardless of his or her ethnicity or language. Everyone would be guaranteed freedom, equality, and protection under this new constitution."

Suddenly, Bari heard loud voices. He looked at the expressions of all the men around the table. Some feared what they would lose if they supported this new constitution. Others smiled at the inclusiveness of the document. For the next three hours, Johannes answered questions from every leader except Kefa Dalmar, who remained silent.

After several hours had passed, the room felt hot and crowded to Johannes. The men at the end of the table discussed Johannes proposed visit to the town of Negele in two weeks. He was going to visit with the students beaten in the riot. Johannes had planned to take Mendi, the leader of the UN security who stood at the door.

A low voice caught the attention of Bari's distracted ear. Turning his head, Bari heard a shifty-eyed man, seated near him ask Kefa Dalmar the time of Johannes' arrival in Negele.

"He will be presented with a surprise in Negele," Kefa Dalmar said in a whisper while he stared into space stroking his chin. The gleam in his eyes made Bari feel a danger he could not see.

Chapter 16

A convoy of UN security jeeps and trucks preceded Johannes' bulletproof SUV down the red rocky highlands leading to the town of Negele. Johannes had carefully prepared for his visit to the victims of the riot. He wanted to give them hope about enrolling in the University.

Bari had reported Dalmar's disturbing conversation to General Matobe after the conference. The General wisely prepared for an attack by Dalmar and his men. He and his men had patrolled the outskirts of Negele every night for the past week and knew what to expect. The General's security vehicles led the way followed by Johannes' SUV and UN forces following in the rear.

Kefa Dalmar watched the convoy from a distance. As the convoy came closer to the town, he and his renegades came out of nowhere and attacked.

Suddenly, Johannes heard gunshots and screams coming from innocent civilians caught in the middle of the attack. General Motabe stopped his jeep and commanded on a two way radio for Johannes driver and the UN forces in the rear to retreat.

The General and his men drove through a furious whirlwind of red dust to fight back. He stopped on a cliff outside the edge of the township and pulled out his powerful binoculars, adjusting them to focus in on Dalmar. “As I thought,” he spoke into his radio to Johannes and his men. “It’s that Devil Dalmar and his murdering renegades.”

Thick black smoke darkened the sky as homes and buildings burned with a fierce intensity. A young woman ran from a doorway holding an infant in one hand and a toddler by the other. She screamed for the toddler to run faster to keep up, but the child let go of her hand. Seconds later, with a horrified look on her face, the woman watched as a jeep full of Dalmar’s soldiers ran over her child, crushing her little body into a limp corpse.

A loud blast came from a soldier firing an automatic AK-47 weapon at General Motabe and his men. Hundreds of Dalmar’s men fired automatic rifles. In the middle of the firefight a crying child fell to the ground. A decrepit old man tried to run across the street leaning on his cane. He wasn’t fast enough; a bullet hit him in the head.

General Motabe drove his men closer to the renegades. He threw a grenade into one of the jeeps. Seconds later, a quick round of bullets fired back within inches of his head, blowing dust and pebbles into his eyes. The General and his men jumped out of jeeps, shielding themselves with the doors. The General pulled out his firearm and began shooting back. He called for more support from the rear forces. Within minutes, he heard the sound of Johannes and the rear troops, firing rounds of ammunition at the renegades.

Johannes pulled out his firearm, rolled out of his SUV and crawled over to the General.

"Prince Johannes, you were supposed to be killed in this attack today," General Motabe said through the chaos.

"Hand me your binoculars," Johannes demanded.

The General handed them to him while still shooting his firearm.

Johannes looked through the binoculars and saw a small toddler of about two or three wandering in the street crying. He had to save the child's life. "I'm going into the town to help," Johannes said to the General.

"No. Your grace. This fight is too dangerous."

Johannes ignored General Motabe. He looked through his binoculars and saw corpses of innocent women and children lying everywhere. Taking the lead, Johannes told his men to cover him. He expertly squirmed on his belly down the hill to try to rescue the child. Once he and his troops were on the edge of the town, Johannes ran for shelter behind buildings until he reached the crying child. He swooped him up in his arms dodging bullets aimed at him. He threw the child into an open doorway. Closing the door, Johannes turned around to face the barrel of a gun. He was shot once in the chest.

When Kefa Dalmar saw the UN security troops advancing toward the township, he ordered his men to retreat. His renegades fled the scene.

After the firefight ended, all General Motabe could see was dust, smoke, and corpses. He ran into the building where he'd last seen Johannes and broke the door down. He rushed to Johannes whom he had assumed was dead. He turned Johannes over and pulled out sobbing child. He felt Johannes' wrist for a pulse. Although weak, he was still alive. He tore off the tail of his shirt and plugged up the blood gushing out of Johannes' chest wound.

"Hurry up and get in here!" The General barked to his men standing outside. "Tend to his wounds," The General commanded as he called for medics on his radio. A minute later, two medics drove up in a jeep with medical supplies and stopped the bleeding. They took Johannes' limp body into the vehicle and rushed him to the nearest hospital in the next town. Later in the evening he was transferred to the Black Lion Hospital in Addis Ababa.

***

The fighting in Ethiopia had finally come to an end. Several months had passed since Johannes had been released from the hospital. Parliament had voted in favor of his amendments. Johannes along with key government officials converted the old political system into one with a new set of guidelines all supported except for one.

His chief opponent was Kefa Dalmar. He was a man driven by sheer power and greed. He would never accept the new constitution, or stop fighting. Several months after the implementation of the constitution, Dalmar fed his troops rhetoric based on what they had endured under the old system. But his vicious words no longer worked. Before fleeing the country to Uganda, Dalmar vowed vengeance would be his one day. "Prince Johannes may win this conflict," he said to his loyal men, "but he will one day lose his life."

After being shot in the chest in Negele, Johannes survived numerous assassination attempts. The next one occurred inside a restaurant in Addis Ababa. A jeep drove by, firing rounds at Johannes and Bari, but no one was hurt. The second attempt happened when a car bomb went off in Johannes' limousine killing the hired driver instantly. Ali was conveniently visiting relatives in Mogadishu. After that incident, Johannes took Mendi and his UN security wherever he went.

Weary of assassination attempts, Johannes commanded General Motabe and the UN security forces to find out where this threat was coming from. Despite the heavy UN security Johannes still suffered numerous attempts on his life. His father encouraged him to leave the country again for a much needed vacation.

Johannes and Bari flew to Uganda while the UN enforced the new constitution. The day after Johannes arrived in Uganda; he received a wire informing him Dalmar had been captured. The civil war had ended, and the new constitution was now the foundation of Ethiopian law. Johannes and Bari celebrated all night long.

Chapter 17

Shana looked at the emerald ring on her finger as she sat in her office. She didn't know why she kept the ring on. Maybe to keep from losing the precious stone, she told herself. If she were honest, she would admit she still wore the ring because she never stopped loving Johannes. The memory of the day he gave her the ring to her crossed her mind. She remembered how she had begged Johannes to take his grandmother's ring back, but he wouldn't. He told her, as long as she kept the ring, fate would one day bring them back together. She looked at the ring and realized more than ever how much she missed him. Tears slowly found a path down her cheeks as she thought about Johannes. From the beginning, he treated her with loving kindness. Since time had passed, she could see in hindsight she had made the greatest mistake of her life when she pushed him away. Her life was rich living in Kenya and learning about the culture and people, but the hard cold fact remained—there was no substitute for Johannes.

Before she began to work on her financial reports, she turned the radio on to listen to the morning news. An announcement came on the air: "The civil war in Ethiopia has ended, and a new constitution has been adopted."

Johannes' image immediately came to her mind.

She quickly turned up the volume and listened as the announcer commended the success of Prince Johannes and how he brought peace to the country by amending the constitution. The announcer reported Prince Johannes had been nominated for a Nobel Peace Prize.

"Nobel Peace Prize?" Shana whispered. She sat with a stunned look on her face as she listened to the announcer. The news brought out deep emotions. Uncontrollable tears rolled down her face. She knew Johannes was a good man. His love showed in his works and deeds. All he ever did was try to love her, but she pushed him away. She never knew Johannes was such a great man. She knew she was the biggest fool who'd ever lived.

***

Friday's were hectic at the embassy because everyone wanted to leave early for the weekend. Shana patiently waited for lingering customers to leave. At four thirty the building was empty and she headed for home.

On the way home, she couldn't get Johannes out of her mind. She thought about them racing down the beach and going to see the Dance Theater of Harlem in Los Angeles. The memory of the day when he gave her his mother's ring, crossed her mind. She shook her head to try and clear her thoughts. Those days were gone, she'd thought. She had her chance, and she blew it. No sense in crying over spilled milk, she thought.

After arriving home, she took a long soothing bath and dressed for dinner. Layla had prepared another one of her scrumptious meals, but Shana wasn't hungry. Her mind remained on Johannes. She went up to her room and slipped on a silk nightie, climbed into bed and cried herself to sleep.

It was seven forty-five in the evening when the telephone rang, jolting her out of a deep sleep. She counted the rings from under the covers, wondering who her caller could be. If Dr. Burnham, called to invite himself over for dinner, she would have to come up with an excuse because she didn't want to be bothered. On the fifth ring, she answered the call.

"Good evening, Shana."

A sharp sensation gripped the pit of Shana's stomach at the sound of Johannes voice.

"Johannes?" A soft gasp escaped her mouth.

"Yes, My Dove," he said in his smooth voice. "It is good to hear your voice again."

She could feel the rapid beat of her heart. Her voice caught in her throat. "Johannes," was all she could say."

"How are you doing?" His voice, deep and sensual, sent a ripple of awareness through Shana.

Tears flowed, but words wouldn't come through

Shana's mouth for a long moment. "Johannes, I'm happy to hear your voice. Where are you?"

"I am at the airport." The sound of Shana's trembling voice tore at his heart. He understood Shana better than she understood herself. "I'm on my way over to sweep you off of your feet and take you away to Uganda for the weekend. Give me your address."

Shana gave her address to him, speaking softly into the phone.

"I'll be over in 20 minutes." He ended the call before she could reject his offer.

Shana couldn't believe this was happening. She jumped up out of bed, combed her hair, and found something to wear. Minutes later, Johannes was knocking at the door. She opened the door to him standing tall, regal and handsome in his white shirt and tan trousers.

"Johannes," Shana cried out before walking into his arms.

He held Shana in his embrace whispering her name. Tears of joy ran down Shana's face as Johannes kissed her lips. He clamped his arms around her waist, claiming her body for his own. She reached her arms around his neck, closing her eyes, and abandoning herself to the experience once again of kissing the man she loved. His hands moved over her back, hips and breasts sending flames of passion through her body.

"My God, Shana, you do not know the power you have over me. I have not been able to get you out of my mind since I last saw you. Your spirit has haunted me every single day. I could not let another day pass without seeing you."

His hand moved slowly over her, exploring the softness of her body. All the while, he pressed her harder and harder against his taut, muscular frame. "Shana, Shana," he whispered. He moved his lips from hers, and kissed her neck, shoulder and mouth.

"Shana, I love you."

Tears filled Shana's eyes once again as Johannes said the words she longed to hear. But, she knew she didn't deserve Johannes after the way she had treated him.

"Johannes, I missed you terribly. I'm sorry for treating you badly. How can you ever forgive me?" she whispered. Passion raced through her body like a flash of white lightning, making her feel weak in the knees. "I had no consideration for your feelings, I was selfish, and you were kind to me...and..."

He took her by the hand and walked inside to the sofa. "Everything is fine, My Dove." He pulled her down next to him. "I understand you better than you think. You needed more time."

He raised her face in the palms of his hands and spoke to her seriously. "I always knew you would be my wife. I've never doubted you would be my wife since the day I saw you in walk in coffeehouse. I've never felt this way about anyone before. Our love was meant to be. Come with me to Lake Victoria, in Uganda for the weekend," he said as he reluctantly released her.

"I would, but aren't you supposed to be going to Sweden to receive your Nobel Peace Prize?" Shana smiled sweetly.

Johannes smiled and said, "How did you know?"

"I heard it on the news this morning." Shana's eyes were as soft as the wind.

Pulling Shana closer to him he said, "Well that trip is not until the end of the month. I am hoping you will accompany me."

Shana thought about her responsibilities. "But what about my job? I can't leave and take off like this?"

"Yes you can. Why don't you take a short leave of absence? I'm sure your co-workers can cover for you." Johannes said.

Shana's eyes widened in hopeful anticipation. "I have never been to Lake Victoria, but I hear the lake is a beautiful place."

"Not as beautiful as you, My Dove."

"This is all happening too fast Johannes," she stated in a concerned voice.

"Don't worry. You are going to go upstairs and dress for dinner. When we return, you will pack your bags, and we will take my plane to Uganda."

Shana had gone to bed feeling depressed and lonely, and now hours later she was taking a weekend trip with the man she loved to Lake Victoria. She thought about the lyrics to a song she'd heard Beyoncé sing. She started humming the lyrics to the song as she went upstairs to change.

Still oppressively hot outside, Shana decided to wear a white halter dress and high-heeled sandals. She accessorized her outfit with silver hoop earrings and an elephant charm bracelet. She let her curly hair hang loose and free falling gently down her back.

When she descended the ebony staircase, Johannes was reminded of the first time he saw her. She looked as beautiful now as she did then. He smiled at her as she walked into his embrace once again. He kissed her softly on the lips and told her how beautiful she looked. He opened the front door for her, and they walked to his limousine where Ali was standing.

Shana smiled when she saw Ali's familiar face. Ali's face remained expressionless when he saw her, but then greeted her, after opening the car door for her. Shana felt slightly uncomfortable as she passed Ali to get into the car as if his eyes held a dangerous secret. She looked up at his face and saw him staring straight ahead. Must be nerves, she thought.

They dined at downtown Nairobi's Kilimanjaro Supper Club, famous for international cuisine and soft, romantic music. When they walked in, Shana noticed the musician was wearing a long white muslin outfit and a matching cap. He sat on a mat with his legs folded, holding a stringed instrument resembling an Indian sitar. He began to play the most harmonious music she'd ever heard.

Shana and Johannes talked in great detail about what they had been doing since they had left the United States, as they dined on baked fish, curry rice and spicy green salad. Shana gasped when Johannes told her about all of the attempts on his life. He smiled when she told him about how she had established a field office at the Embassy and made a positive contribution to the community. He was also happy to hear how much she had missed him.

After dinner, they took a walk along the moonlit pier behind the restaurant.

"Shana, I want to ask you something." Johannes took Shana in his arms and kissed her tenderly, then knelt on one knee, holding both of her hands in his.

"Shana, will you marry me?"

Shana stared at him through glistening eyes and said, "Yes."

Chapter 18

Kampala, Uganda

The mist from Lake Victoria rose like a blanket of netting, cooling the intense heat of the early morning. Johannes and Shana were fully clothed entwined in each other's embrace, waiting to greet the sunrise. Johannes fought the urge to make love to Shana all through the night. They had decided to sleep outside under the stars, also under the watchful eye of his security. Johannes pulled himself up from underneath the blanket and stood to stretch.

Shana squirmed under the blanket, noticing Johannes' warm body next to hers was gone. She slid the blanket away from her face and saw Johannes standing facing the lake.

"Good morning, My Dove." He bent down and cupped her face in the palms of his hands.

"Good morning to you," Shana replied. Her thoughts centered on the previous night. Johannes had chartered a plane from Nairobi to the Entebbe airport in Uganda carrying Shana, security guards, house workers, and officials. All of these people prevented Shana and Johannes from having any intimate privacy on the plane. They'd arrived at the lake house late, but neither of them felt sleepy.

They took a blanket and walked along the water front, talking and laughing as security guards followed them at a discreet distance. Finally they both decided to spend the night right where they were. Shana had wanted Johannes to make love to her on the beach, but felt too embarrassed to ask. Johannes didn't want to make love to Shana until they had some privacy and Shana felt completely at ease with him. He wanted her first time to be special.

Shana decided to refocus her mind on the present. She could have sworn she heard Johannes praying while he was standing up looking out at the lake. She tilted her head and asked in an inquisitive voice, "Do you always pray in the morning?"

"Yes. I do."

"What religion are you?"

"Ethiopian Orthodox Christian."

"I'm a Christian too. AME Methodist."

Johannes helped Shana up and then picked up the blanket. He brushed off some sand from Shana's arm and embraced her kissing her on the forehead.

"Come on, we should get back."

As they made their way back to the lake house followed at a reasonable distance by his security, Shana took in the beauty of the area. The flowers had a unique look she'd never seen. The red and pink flowers exhibited a three-dimensional effect with their deep, rich, intense colors. Lush foliage, huge plants, and exotic trees lined the up-hill path they took. Halfway to the beach house and exhausted from climbing the steep hill, Shana stopped to wipe her brow. She turned around and gasped. She saw the most beautiful sight she'd ever seen. Glorious Lake Victoria looked like a prehistoric body of water that could have existed before the dawn of humans. Johannes stood behind her and wrapped his arms around her shoulders. He understood what she felt. He felt that way too. He was delighted to see she appreciated the amazing view of the lake, as he had hoped.

"We are in Kololo Hills," he said softly into Shana's ear as he savored the moment. After they rested, they continued on their journey.

When they reached the lake house, a young man greeted them. Johannes began speaking to him in Swahili. Johannes told the young man this was his fiancé, pointing to Shana. The young man smiled. Johannes brought him over to meet Shana.

"Shana, I would like you to meet David, he takes care of the lake house." Johannes introduced him in English. Shana replied in Swahili. She found out David was a student. He told her he had prepared their breakfast.

Johannes raised his eyebrows. He had completely forgotten that Shana spoke Swahili. David was all smiles.

Once they ate their breakfast, Johannes showed Shana her room, which was light and airy. He was still determined to wait until she was ready for intimacy, before making love to her. They both slept in separate rooms for the remainder of the day.

Early the following morning Johannes took Shana on a tour of the lake on a private yacht. They dined on grilled shrimp and salad. Johannes also invited Bari and his girlfriend Imani, who spoke French, and two other couples. Shana held a short, but interesting conversation with Imani and the other couples when she found out they all spoke French. Shana excused herself and walked the deck of the yacht to enjoy the spectacular view.

She stood at the tip of the vessel, leaning against the rails with the wind blowing through her hair. The warm air felt good against her skin. She admitted to herself she had never seen a sight as majestic as Lake Victoria. The waterfalls alone were ten times greater than Niagara Falls. Johannes walked up to her and put his arm around her waist and pointed out with his free hand places where he and his sisters played as children on family vacations. Shana fell in love with one particular lagoon surrounded with white sand and tall windswept trees. Johannes assured her the lagoon was the best possible place for swimming.

“As a young man,” he said solemnly, “my father purchased several hundred acres of land scattered around Lake Victoria. But the Ugandan government forced him to sell most of his land to wealthy Ugandan citizens. As the area began growing into a private playground for wealthy Ugandan’s, my father lost most of his land except for this lake house our family owns today. The lake house has been our family vacation retreat since I was born.”

Shortly before noon, Johannes had security turn the yacht around and head back to the house. Before arriving, Bari invited Johannes over to his place for a barbecue the next day. After Shana and Imani prepared a light snack, and ate by the pool. They were conversing contentedly, when Bari and Johannes joined them.

“Did you tell Shana about the barbecue tomorrow?” Bari asked Johannes. “You know I will be very disappointed if you two do not show up. I want to show off Shana to our friends.”

“I’d love to come,” Shana said.

Everyone spent the remainder of the day relaxing and enjoying Johannes’ and Bari’s tales of childhood adventures sounded like something out of a story book.

The next day, shortly after noon, Shana took a nap before going to the barbecue. She lay in bed daydreaming about Johannes tender kisses. She wondered what he was doing at the moment. Probably talking with Bari, she thought.

She closed her eyes, and a warm sensation flowed through her body. But then a chilling thought occurred to her. She could lose her life as an innocent bystander with all of the assassination attempts on Johannes' life. She'd found out life as a royal was extremely dangerous. She fluffed her pillow and accepted this could indeed happen, but she was not afraid. She also accepted the fact that his royal duties would probably take up most of his time, which was fine with her. Was this the price to pay, she reasoned, for being in love with Johannes? If so, she didn't care.

Shana woke up from her nap a couple of hours later, refreshed and ready for the barbecue. She showered, piled her hair on top of her head, and slipped into a loose-fitting cotton blouse and linen slacks. She packed a swimsuit, towel, and other necessities in a straw bag. She stepped into a pair of sandals, and went down to the living room.

"Hello," Shana greeted Johannes softly.

Johannes was relaxing in a chair with his legs stretched out on an ottoman.

She walked over and stood behind him and gave him an upside down kiss.

“You’re right on time,” Johannes assured her kissing her again.

Shana’s heart began to throb when he pulled her onto his lap caressing her. He stared deeply into her eyes, rubbing the side of her face with the back of his hand and kissed her neck. Shana sat breathless in his embrace until he let her go. He took her by the hand and said, “Come on. Let’s go.”

Shana followed him like a little puppy.

After they walked outside, Johannes opened the car door where Ali was sitting. “So how are you enjoying your weekend?” Johannes asked, waiting for her to settle into the car.

Shana was still in a daze. She couldn’t believe how quickly everything was happening. “I’m enjoying every moment,” she answered.

Ali drove down a narrow paved road until they reached the long driveway leading to Bari’s villa. Johannes security followed. “Since our excursion yesterday, I’ve fallen in love with Lake Victoria, especially your lovely lagoon.”

“Oh yes, the lagoon,” Johannes chuckled. “It’s the perfect place for skinny dipping.”

Shana’s eyes lit up. She was shocked to hear Africans skinny dipped too. They both were laughing as Ali pulled into the driveway of Bari’s villa. They got out of the car and followed the scent of grilled meat. They found their hosts, Bari, and Imani, conversing with a small group of people on the side of the house.

"Hello you two," Bari said, getting up to introduce Shana to a group of about five couples and lots of children running around all over the place. "We thought you had changed your mind and decided not to come," Bari joked, holding Imani by the shoulder.

"We would not disappoint you," Johannes said, shaking his friend's hand.

Johannes stood to face the crowd. "This is Shana Zachary, my future bride," Johannes announced proudly.

Sounds of applause and sighs could be heard.

"It is a pleasure to meet you," one young lady said as she came up to personally introduce herself to Shana. Bari introduced everyone else to Shana individually.

"Let me show you where to change," Imani said to Shana in French. She took Shana's hand, leading the way to a changing room by the swimming pool. Imani was a short small-boned petite woman with a pretty face and a friendly smile.

Johannes and Bari changed into their swimming trunks and joined the others at the pool while

Johannes' security looked on.

Shana wore a navy blue and white nautical looking one-piece swimsuit and a matching navy sarong. A young male server came over and handed Shana a fruit punch served in a coconut hull after she found herself a seat in front of the pool. Shana shifted in her seat when she caught sight of Johannes in his turquoise swimming trunks on the other side of the pool. She'd never seen him without a shirt. She had no idea that he had such a muscular build. She watched him dive into the pool and come up right in front of her.

"Come join me. The water feels good," he said through glistening white teeth and water dripping from his sexy body.

Shana shook her head. "No, I never learned how to swim."

"Come in. I will teach you."

Shana slid into the water.

Johannes held her around her waist and gave her a big kiss. Sighs and applause greeted them both, from the crowd of couples standing around the poolside enjoying their drinks. The crowd was happy for the future bride and groom.

Johannes' stomach began to growl, "Is the barbecue ready?" he shouted across the pool to Bari.

“Give me thirty minutes,” Bari answered waving his hand.

“You and Shana must begin the first dance,” Bari yelled as he turned up the music louder.

Johannes and Shana chose not to dance, but swam and played in the pool for about thirty minutes until they were both exhausted. Afterward, Johannes took Shana by the hand and led her to the sun deck where others were beginning to dance. Wrapping both of his arms around her waist, he began to move and sway to the hypnotic beat of the music.

Shana rested her head against Johannes wide chest and felt a warm, good feeling once again. She fit like a glove in his arms. She folded her arms around his neck and listened contentedly to the soft song he sang into her ear. She didn’t care if she couldn’t understand the words to his song. Feeling his lean, muscular body pressed against hers, as she inhaled the sweet fragrance of his body was enough for her. Johannes spotted one of his good friend’s coming through security at the gate. When the music stopped, Johannes pulled away from Shana slowly. “Why don’t you talk to Imani for a minute? I need to do something” he said, looking deep into her eyes.

Although her heartbeat was erratic, and she felt a little shaky, she agreed. “May I have some water, please?” she asked a passing waiter. He handed her a bottle of water. Shana found a chair by Imani and sat down.

"Are you enjoying yourself?" Imani asked Shana.

"Oui, Tre Bien," Shana replied.

A group of guests beckoned Shana to join them in a card game, which she declined. Shana was terrible at card games. Desiring some quiet time, she found a chaise lounge by the pool underneath a shady tree. She leaned back and closed her eyes.

"Are you enjoying yourself?" she heard someone ask in English. She opened her eyes and saw Bari's pleasant face smiling down at her.

Shana lifted herself up on her elbows. "I'm having a great time Bari. Have you seen Johannes, he seemed to have disappeared."

"Oh yes," Bari replied. "The last time I saw him he was talking to an old friend of ours." Shana looked beyond Bari's shoulders and saw Johannes talking to a middle-aged, bald man. She pointed to the chair next to her and asked Bari to join her for a while.

Shana loved to hear Johannes and Bari's childhood adventures. She wanted to know what unseen forces convicted Johannes to believe in his causes.

Bari sat peacefully in the chair, looking up at the sun was about to set.

"Bari, tell me about Johannes. What motivates him to believe in his convictions?" Shana asked.

Bari crossed his legs and folded his hands behind his head, smiling at Shana.

Shana adjusted the back of her chaise lounge and sat up to hear the answer to her question.

"Johannes is a great man, you know. The force motivating him the most is his love for his country." Bari said, giving her a serious look. "Do you know how long a human can go without food?" he asked. He answered his question. "Three weeks, maybe a month." He paused for a moment. "One time Johannes fasted to prove we could endure the famine plaguing our country. After his fast was over, he sat in a wheelchair before the people on national television and told us never to underestimate ourselves, but to rely on faith to see us through challenging times. After that, the people were able to endure the famine. Some died, of course, but he gave us all a sense of hope that sustained us, something we will never forget."

Shana's eyes watered as she listened to Bari. She was truly touched by this story about Johannes. She knew Johannes was way beyond her in his noble way of thinking. He was a true leader, she thought. "Tell me about his family," she asked with a soft voice, then turned around and saw Imani poking a fork at the barbecue, turning the meat over.

Bari leaned forward in his chair clasping his hands between his knees. “I will give you a brief introduction to his family history if you promise me you will learn about our culture and history yourself,” he said in a fatherly tone.

Shana crossed her heart with her index finger and smiled at Bari. “I promise.”

“Do you know Johannes took a beating for me when we were both boys?” Bari reminisced with glassy eyes. “Yes, he did,” he spoke softly, lowering his eyes. “We had been out playing soccer all day when several boys came to our field. They were bigger than us, and they asked if they could play. I jumped up and told them we did not want to play with them. They pushed me down for the insult and attempted to take our ball. I jumped up again and repeated my statement. Even though they were all bigger than us, we all began fighting. I was getting hit hard and Johannes told me to run. I did, as a coward and the boys took all of their anger out on him. They beat him to a bloody pulp.” He stood up. “I can tell you from experience Johannes possesses a pure heart, and would easily give up his life for anyone he loves.”

Bari looked up at the sky, as though he could find answers to such unconditional love, he found the setting sun.

Imani announced the barbecue was ready. Shana and Bari met Johannes and Imani at a long table and feasted on grilled fish and shrimp. Afterward, Johannes and Shana said goodbye to the other guests and walked away toward the road with security following.

They walked along the narrow paved road, which was bordered on both sides by thick foliage. Shana could hear an occasional rustle in the underbrush, and then she saw an iguana run by quickly. They both walked slowly and peacefully into the sunset.

The next morning as they ate their breakfast on the verandah, they agreed this would be a lovely place to exchange their vows. Shana wanted to get married in the spring. Johannes explained the custom was for all royal marriages to take place in the Ethiopian Orthodox Church. Shana agreed even though she'd been raised in the AME Methodist Church.

Johannes convinced Shana to take a temporary leave of absence to spend more time with him in Uganda. Shana was completely unprepared for Johannes' suggestion. Yet, she couldn't deny her feelings for Johannes or her gut feeling this was the right thing to do. She agreed to take an extended leave of absence.

Later in the afternoon, Johannes didn't want Shana to hear his conversations with his father. He told her he had some business to take care of in town. Instead, he went over to Bari's house and called his father. Johannes had a long talk with his father, asking for his blessing on his marriage.

"But she is not a royal." His father complained.

"She is not Ethiopian either." Johannes said.

"You know how much this goes against our tradition," his father said.

"Father," Johannes pleaded. "I love her. She means the world to me. You have the power to accept her. Traditions can change."

Johannes happiness meant everything to his father. He was happy Johannes had finally found a woman to marry. He thought about his son's choice long and hard and realized he trusted his son's judgment. "My son, if you love this woman and want to marry her, then you have my blessing."

"Thank you, father. You won't regret your decision." He ended the call and discussed his father's blessing with Bari who had heard the entire conversation.

After a while, Johannes began making more telephone calls. First, he called Rebecca and told her to make preparations for a royal wedding. He instructed her to call Shana's Aunt, her friend Lauren, and Mr. Withers. He told Rebecca she could get all of the telephone numbers by contacting Lauren Washington in San Francisco, California.

Next, he told Rebecca to hire a wedding consultant, prepare guest rooms at his family's estate, and make travel arrangements for all of Shana's friends and family to attend the wedding.

Later in the day Rebecca called Lauren who was asleep. When Rebecca told Lauren the news, all she heard was tears of joy. "Remember," Rebecca said. "This is a surprise for Miss Shana."

"I am happy for Shana," Lauren confessed. "She told me all about Prince Johannes."

"I am calling because I am going to need your help," Rebecca said.

"What do you needt me to do?" Lauren asked happily.

"I need you to give me a list of names and addresses for Miss Shana's friends, relatives, and co-workers. You may tell them the good news, but make sure they have updated passports and be sure to tell them to keep this a secret from Shana. Prince Johannes wants her to be surprised on their wedding day. I will contact you later about travel, lodging and the details of the wedding."

"How is Shana doing? I miss her a lot, but if this is going to be a secret, I guess I shouldn't contact her.

"Smart girl." Rebecca replied. "Shana is fine. You will have a chance to talk to her as much as you want when you come to the wedding."

Lauren would soon be traveling to Africa. "I will get in touch with everyone as soon as I can and I will send you a list."

"Shana was right when she said you were a good friend." Rebecca thanked her and ended the call.

Bari listened to Johannes make telephone calls informing his sisters and other family members of the good news. When Johannes finished his calls, Bari came over and gave him a handshake and a smile. "Congratulations, my friend."

"Thank you Bari." Johannes stayed a while longer but left before dusk. He didn't want to leave Shana alone by herself for too long.

***

Late in the evening, Shana tossed and turned in her bed. She could not sleep. Feelings of deep love for Johannes drew her away from her room. She was ready. Pulling the covers away from her body, she entered into Johannes' room and stood before him. Touched by the serene look on his sleeping face, she slid into his bed and breathed his name in a soft whisper.

Awaking out of a deep sleep, Johannes' eyes opened at the sound of Shana's voice. He immediately smiled and gently pulled her into his embrace. She buried her face against the muscles of his bare chest. Instinctively knowing she was ready, he gave Shana a passionate kiss sending her into a spiral of heady sensations. His hands slipped down to her thighs, bringing her closer to his body. As his grip tightened, his appetite for her love became more ravenous. He wrapped his arms around her midriff and explored the hollows of her back. Shivers of delight followed his magic touch. Shana's mind whirled like a tornado over her emotions. Feelings of deep love and intense warmth overcame her. Johannes' heart rang with happiness as he felt Shana responding to his love without inhibitions. He returned her feverish kisses pressing hotly against his mouth. His hands softly caressed her body, touching her in ways that took her breath away.

Johannes removed his pajama bottoms, flinging them carelessly aside. He pressed his body against her soft flesh that seared blazing heat into his core. His hand seared a path down her abdomen and onto her thighs. His gentle touch sent currents of desire through Shana. His lips teased a taut dark nipple as his hands searched for pleasure points. One hand slid down her taut stomach to the swell of her hips. She curled into the curve of his body. He paused, whispering his love for each part of her body. She gasped as he lowered his body over hers skin to skin. He pressed her down into the bed, and for a brief moment the room spun before Shana's eyes. She cried out in pain, and then responded fully to his rhythm. He whispered into her ear, kissing her where he could feel the rapid beat of her heart. Her impatience grew to explosive proportions. His expert touch sent her to even higher levels of ecstasy. Together they found the tempo that bound their bodies together. She shamelessly cried out in sweet agony as Johannes reached the peak of delight, branding her with his love.

Contentment and peace flowed between them. Shana finally knew what making love felt like. Her fear of intimacy had gradually vanished. She never even noticed her fear was gone. Like the petals of a rose, Johannes had peeled off her fears, one by one until nothing remained. He had conquered her mind, and then her heart, but most of all he had conquered her tormented soul.

Chapter 19

Early Monday morning Johannes summoned Ali to take him into town to take care of some unfinished business. Ali informed Johannes he was suffering from a bad stomach virus and wasn't able to drive. Johannes summoned Mendi to find him a driver.

Engaged with security training, Mendi appointed two senior security officers to drive Johannes into town. The driver had been traveling down the long narrow road for about fifteen minutes, when a black sedan pulled in front of them on the opposite side of the road, blocking the road, forcing the driver to stop the car. Johannes looked through the front window of his SUV trying to get a better view and saw two heavily armed men dressed in military clothing get out of the black sedan firing automatic weapons at the driver. Fortunately the SUV was bulletproof.

"Kefa Dalmar," Johannes growled underneath his breath.

"Get down, Your Grace." The driver and the other security officer pulled out their firearms and began firing back through open windows at the two soldiers.

Johannes lowered his head and pulled a knife

from underneath the seat where he kept weapons hidden for such occasions. He tucked the knife into the back of his pants, then opened the back door and jumped out. One of the renegades threw a live grenade through the window, killing both security officers. One soldier ran around to the side of the car and shot Johannes in the arm, deliberately not killing him. Then hit Johannes in the head with the butt of his firearm, leaving him in a crumpled heap.

When Johannes woke up, he had trouble comprehending where he was. His head pounded with a silent fury he'd experienced once before. His body ached, and his mouth felt as dry as the Sahel Desert. He tried to stand and put forth an attempt at figuring out what had happened but fell again into unconsciousness.

When he woke again, he lay still, realizing half of the pain he was experiencing came from tight chains holding him captive around his feet and hands. He had been chained to a wall in a dark, damp, cement cellar. He gagged at the stench of decayed human urine. He hung his head down and fell again into an unconscious state.

***

It was ten o'clock and Shana was waking up when she realized Johannes was not lying next to her. She read a note he had left her.

"My Dove, I have gone into town for a while to take care of some business. I will be back shortly. I love you, Johannes."

Shana smiled to herself as she read the note. She popped up out of bed humming a delightful song to herself. She had never been this happy in her life. Walking into the bathroom, she turned on the shower and undressed. She was about to step into the shower when the telephone rang. She slipped on a lightweight pale blue robe and went into the bedroom to answer the call.

"You'll never marry Johannes, I will kill you both before that day ever comes."

Shana stood over the bed with her mouth wide open.

"Who is this? Who is this? Answer me? Who is this?" No one answered. The caller ended the call.

She knew Celine's voice. Her body began trembling, and her hands wouldn't stop shaking. Sitting down on the side of the bed, she tried to remember exactly what Celine had said. She couldn't remember.

She walked back into the bathroom to continue with her shower, then her phone rang again, stopping her midway. She turned around and walked back toward the bedroom, dreading to hear

Celine's voice again. The phone rang three times, before she answered the call.

"Don't even think about telling Johannes about this call. Leave him now! Or you will both die."

Fear raced through Shana's body like a bolt of electricity. She immediately phoned Bari and told him about Celine's threats. He calmed her down and told her he would be right over.

When he arrived, he questioned Shana, trying to make some sense of the whole ordeal. Celine called and said if I didn't leave, Johannes and I would both die."

"Celine is a lunatic from Martinique." Bari stated flatly. "Show me the note," he said as he walked toward the parlor window. He looked through the window as he sat down and could see someone walking in the guest house. He read the note and arched his eyebrows. "How did Johannes get into town today, because I saw Ali walking around in the guest house?"

Shana shrugged her shoulders. "I thought Ali drove him."

They both walked into the courtyard leading to the guest house and knocked on the door. At first he didn't answer, but after Bari's persistent knocking and banging, Ali opened the door wearing a cotton robe.

"We need to ask you some questions at once," Bari said in a demanding voice.

Ali gave him a perplexed look. "What do you want to know?"

"Why didn't you take Johannes into town this morning?"

"I informed, His Grace I was feeling ill with some virus. Two of Mendi's security officers took him into town." Ali said without skipping a beat.

"Well for your information, Prince Johannes is missing," Bari said angrily.

Ali stood with a blank look, his hair uncombed and his face unwashed.

"Come, Shana, we need to investigate this further." Bari dismissed Ali.

They walked into the courtyard. With a tense look on her face, Shana said to Bari, "I can feel in my gut something terrible has happened."

"Tell me again, Celine's exact words," Bari said. "She's crazy enough to follow up on her threats."

Shana thought hard and remembered every word. She repeated the entire conversation word for word. "Tell me more about Celine," Shana asked with an inquisitive look on her face.

Memories crossed her mind of the woman standing in front of the white jaguar arguing with Johannes in Hillsboro. “Does she have long hair?” Shana asked remembering Johannes’ conversation about Celine’s mental illness.

“This woman is very sick, Shana.”

“Yes. I know. Johannes told me all about her, but she is in the United States. Isn’t she?”

“She has enough money to move around anywhere in the world whenever she wants.” Bari said. “I think we should talk to Mendi. He is Johannes’ head of security. I once worked closely with him back home. He will help us.” Bari called Mendi on his cell phone. “In the meantime, you stay here and do not leave this villa. Johannes would kill me if I let anything happen to you.”

Mendi came in from his post on the perimeters of the compound and met Bari and Shana inside the lake house. Bari explained everything to Mendi. They both drove into town following Johannes footsteps.

Shana walked through the courtyard and saw Ali standing by his open window. She quietly walked over to his window and hid behind a bush. She heard him shouting at someone. She gasped when she heard him say the words precious prince. She moved closer to the window to hear the conversation better.

"Don't worry, they won't hurt him." she heard Ali say. "Good. Good. I'll see you soon." She heard Ali end the call and look out the window.

Shana covered her mouth to hold back her gasp. As she suspected, Johannes was in trouble. She was shocked to think Ali could be involved in such a dark deed as kidnapping. Then she thought. Maybe he was talking to Celine. Maybe they were they working together? If so, then where had they taken Johannes? All Shana knew was she needed to find a car quick.

Shana ran into the lake house and got her handbag and some extra cash. She walked down the villa road and saw a taxi driver sitting in a car across the street reading a newspaper. She went over to him and asked him if she could hire him for the entire day. A wide grin spread across his face. She informed the driver to wait until a limousine came down the hill. She instructed the cab driver to follow the limousine closely without getting lost.

***

Meanwhile, Bari Mendi and several security officers drove downtown. On the way, Bari called Johannes' father and informed him about the newest threat to his son.

Bari found out from Johannes father, that Kefa Dalmar had escaped days after he'd been captured.

Once Bari heard this news, he thought Dalmar was behind Johannes' disappearance. He had a lead for Mendi.

Bari knew he couldn't let Shana know about Dalmar, or else she would get them all killed.

He would let Shana think Celine was behind Johannes disappearance. He needed to keep her occupied until he could find Dalmar and have him arrested.

***

After Shana and the taxi driver had been following Ali for an hour, they finally reached the grounds of an old British coffee factory. Shana told the taxi driver to stop. She didn't want to be seen. "We'll wait here until dark."

Several hours later, the sun disappeared and the sky became dusk. "It's time," she told the driver. "Remember, wait here for me even if you have to wait until morning. I'll pay you handsomely." The taxi driver watched her leave and then continued reading his paper.

Shana tiptoed up to the factory warehouse. Silently, she eased up to the ground-floor window and peeped through. She saw Ali talking to two men dressed in military clothing. She could barely hear what they were saying, but she saw they were all drunk sitting at a table. Ali drank from a mug amid cheers from the other two men. He slammed the empty mug on the table and began ranting and raving about the privileged class. “That precious prince in the basement was born with a silver spoon in his mouth,” Ali complained as he watched one of the men slide drunkenly beneath the bench. “I plan to get some of his money for myself.” The two men laughed heartily.

Shana couldn’t believe her ears. How could Ali kidnap Johannes like this? How did he ever get past Johannes tough security background checks? He must have slipped through cracks because he’d been Johannes’ driver for years. She always felt in her gut Ali could not be trusted. She tried to stand on her toes to get a better look, but her foot became lodged between some old railway tracks. She bent down to loosen her shoe and saw a movement through a small storm window. She looked closer but couldn’t see anything in the dusk.

Probably a mouse, she thought. Then the thought occurred to her the movement could be Johannes. If Ali was kidnapping Johannes, he would bring him here in this remote location. Shana took a small flashlight attached to her house keys and pressed the button. She gasped when she looked through the window and saw Johannes chained up against the wall looking almost dead.

She tried to open the window, but the casement was jammed shut from years of disuse. She ran to an entrance farther down the warehouse and tried to open the door but it was locked. She returned to her original position at the window. She stood up and looked at Ali and his men through the top window. She noticed a ring of keys clipped to one of the men's belt.

If I could get those keys. She saw a large piece of lead pipe and knew instantly what she had to do—pick up the pipe, and wait for the man with the keys to come out, and then hit him in the back of the head and unlock the door.

She walked back toward the taxi and tried to use her cell phone, but couldn't get service this far up country. She asked the driver if he had a dispatch radio. He said yes. She asked him if he could call in and tell the dispatcher to call Johannes security because the prince had been kidnapped. The dispatcher was able to contact Mendi and Bari. Shana told them everything, then she gave them her location.

Bari told her to have the taxi driver take her home. He and Mendi would handle the situation. Shana didn't want to risk Johannes' life. She told Bari she would go back to the villa, when she knew all too well she was going back to help Johannes.

The taxi cab driver listened to the dangerous nature of Shana's call. Not wanting to get in the middle of a deadly situation, once Shana was out of his view, he turned around and left the scene. When Shana returned to the warehouse, she picked up the lead pipe and waited behind a thick bush next to the door. She looked through the window and saw the men were in a drunken stupor.

An hour later the guard with the keys came out, singing a song and carrying a plate of food for Johannes. When he walked by the window, Shana leaped from behind the shrub and hit him in the back of his head with all of her strength. He was out like a light.

She swiftly took the keys from his belt and ran to unlock the door, but the door was jammed. She kept turning the key over and over and realized she was wasting time.

One last time, she thought to herself, but that one last time was enough time for Ali to approach her from behind.

"So, the little American princess is trying to save her precious African prince."

Shana gasped, and trembled nervously as she turned her head around to face Ali. He gave her a lusty look and drunkenly grabbed at her in a futile attempt to rip off her blouse. Shana bit his hands.

"Get your hands off of me, you...you kidnapper."

"Careful, Ali warned." With a hard fist, he hit Shana across her face. She fell backward hitting her head against the concrete stairs. She was out cold. He kicked the door open, tied her hands behind her back and threw her limp body in the basement along with Johannes.

"Don't worry, little American princess, I will have a taste of you later."

When Shana woke up, she felt like she'd been hit by a ton of bricks. Though her head ached, the dizziness subsided quickly. She could feel her strength returning. She made an unsuccessful attempt to pull at the rope binding her hands behind her back, but the knot was tied too tight. Once her eyes became accustomed to the darkness of the cellar, she saw Johannes crumpled against a wall and sitting on the concrete floor. "Johannes." She cried out his name in a trembling voice.

"Johannes, Johannes, can you hear me?" She sobbed when she looked at him in his pitiful state. His head was bent down on his bleeding chest and his feet were tucked behind his knees in an awkward position. Then she saw blood dripping from his shirt. The sight was too much for her, but something inside of her fought back the tears. She recited some bible verses and a sudden burst of strength overcame her. She told herself she could get them both out of this mess, or she would die trying. No way, she resolved, would she let life rob her of the love this wonderful man had given her.

She thought she saw something shining on the floor behind Johannes' hip. A piece of broken glass? She crawled on her stomach over to Johannes and said in a low voice. "Don't worry Johannes, we'll get out of this." Yes, it was a piece of glass. If she could get the glass and somehow cut the rope binding her hands together, then she could get free.

After several attempts, she finally picked up the glass, cutting her fingers as she lodged herself against the wall. She rubbed the rope against the glass and after several sawing motions, the rope came apart. Now all she needed to do was get Johannes loose.

"He's chained like a slave," she cried under her breath. The chains did look rather old, she thought. If she could muster up enough strength to pull them out of the wall or, better yet, if she picked at the decaying asphalt cement with the glass, she could eventually weaken the chains and pull them out. She picked and pulled at the asphalt continuously until the chains fell down from the wall. Johannes' arms dropped like those of a dead man.

She held back her tears and listened to his heart. It was still beating. Although his face was purple and drained of color, she examined his arm and saw he had a bullet wound in his upper right chest area. She saw his shirt was soaked with blood. She also saw clotting blood covering a gaping hole in the back of his head. She said a quick prayer and continued with untying his feet. Finally, Johannes was loose. She hid the glass in her belt and tore the tail end of her blouse away to wipe the dried blood off of Johannes and tend to his wounds. She brushed her beloved's hair with her fingers and rocked him gently.

She looked up from Johannes' face and thought she saw Ali walk by the tiny storm window. She quickly placed Johannes' hands behind his back, and ran to her position and held her hands behind her back. She heard the lock turn. Ali walked in and faced her. Shana was relieved when Ali was too drunk to notice Johannes was unchained. Shana looked up to face of her captor. He handed her an unclean mug containing some whiskey. Shana turned her head away.

“What are you going to do with us?” Shana asked Ali.

Without saying a word, he watched her with a lustful eye and then walked closer.

Without warning, he slapped her across her face. Shana’s face burned hotly. She couldn’t reach for her face, otherwise, she would expose her untied hands.

“I’ll ask the questions around here.” Ali barked in a drunken voice.

After that, she lowered her head and remained silent.

“I’ve come to take you outside in case you need to relieve yourself.”

Somehow by his look Shana didn’t think a break was his intention.

Something caught her eye. She saw the silhouettes of men dressed in black slipping through the darkness like Ninjas.

"Um, yes I do have a need to relieve myself." Shana said, now convinced she saw Johannes' security forces moving across the grounds.

One of the officers was about to shoot through the window when Bari pulled his arm down. "Not yet."

Ali scanned Shana's body as he pushed her toward the opened door. "You can relieve yourself, over there," he said pointing to a bush. "But do not try to escape or I will kill you with my bare hands."

Shana walked slowly toward the bush with her hands held behind her back to convince Ali she was still bound. She stood behind the wide bush, shocked Ali didn't try to attack her. She didn't see Bari or the security officers anymore. Where were they?

"What's taking you so long" Ali grunted suspiciously.

"I'll be finished in a minute," Shana said as she reached to remove the glass from her belt. Holding the glass tightly in her hands with her arms still held behind her back, she slowly walked around the bush and faced Ali who stood before her. He was completely unclothed! Shana was shocked. "What are you doing Ali?" Shana asked, pretending she didn't know in an attempt to stall for time.

Ali grabbed her arm and ripped her blouse open, popping off all of the buttons. Shana screamed as loud as she could. She moved her arms from behind her back raising the glass to cut him. But he knock the glass out of her hand, and then lustily grabbed her breasts.

Shana tried to resist his grasp, but he was too strong. His strong arms held her close to him. The putrid odor of his drunken breath nauseated her as he laughed in her face.

"No one can hear you out here."

Shana screamed several times again, louder as his rough hand slid down her back. She begged him, "Please, don't hurt me."

Johannes was awakened by Shana's screams. Groggily he tried to fight his way out of a deep dark void that held him unconscious. He had to save his beloved Shana.

Shana bit Ali's arm when he tried to touch her breasts again. He pulled his arm away, and knocked Shana to the ground. Shana scrambled for the glass. Ali kicked the glass away. His eyes blazed with madness. He whirled around unexpectedly and pinned her to the ground.

"Did you think I was going to let you go?" he snarled. "I will tell you exactly what I'm going to do to you. First I'm going to have my way with you, and then I will let my men have you until they get their fill. We will keep you here until we all tire of you, then I will slit your throat with this piece of glass." He scowled in a voice dripping with hatred.

Out of nowhere a voice cried out. "Stop! You slithering snake," Bari said from behind a gathering of bushes. Ali looked up and saw Bari and Mendi with two security officers pointing rifles right into Ali's face. In the distance Ali saw his men being marched into a UN military truck.

Ali snatched Shana, using her as a human shield. He put the glass to her throat.

"One more step and I'll slit her throat like a pig. Drop your weapons or I kill the girl." Ali barked.

Bari, Mendi and the two security officers stared at each other and watched tears run down the side of Shana's face. Although the security team were crack shots, able to shoot Ali right between the eyes with one shot, Bari didn't want to take a chance with Johannes' beloved. "Put your rifles down men." Bari commanded. The two security officers obeyed.

Ali kept a steady eye on the two security officers and said to Bari and Mendi "You too. Throw your gun over here to me." Bari and Mendi obeyed.

Johannes woke up but images looked blurred. He'd lost a lot of blood, but he'd been through worse. He was determined to save his beloved. He walked over to the opened door and saw what was going on. Ali's back was to him. He picked up the lead pipe near the steps. Mustered up what strength he could, Johannes hit Ali on the back of his head with all of his might. Ali fell to the ground. Johannes fell too.

Shana ran quickly to Johannes' side and held his head in her lap. "Hurry up! Get some help. He's lost a lot of blood," she yelled out to Johannes' security.

Bari commanded the men to put Johannes in the jeep and take him to the nearest hospital several miles away.

Johannes stayed in the hospital for almost a week. Shana had a bed placed next to Johannes'. When she wasn't asleep in her bed, she was watching and waiting on Johannes. Thursday evening, Johannes called out Shana's name. The first thing he saw when he opened his eyes was Shana. Slumped down in a chair next to his bed, she woke up at the sound of her name.

"Shana," he called out her name again.

"Johannes," she cried out. She kissed him on his forehead and all over his face. "Johannes," was all she could say.

"I'm okay Shana. I feel a little soreness in my chest and head, but otherwise I'm fine, I'm a little hungry."

"Hungry." Shana said with tears of joy sliding

down her cheeks. “I’ll get you something to eat.” She called for the doctor. When the doctor arrived, he brought Bari with him. Bari’s eyes lit up when he saw his friend alive and awake. Bari reminded Johannes about Ali’s betrayal and then told him of Celine’s threatening phone calls.

“Ali was behind my kidnapping,” Johannes said.

“I know,” Bari said. Ali confessed he and Celine had been sabotaging your romantic endeavors for years. Celine was intent on destroying your relationship with Shana.

“Ali could have killed us all.” Johannes said angrily.

Shana pulled her chair up closer to his bed and wiped Johannes’ brow, kissing his face. “Don’t worry about Ali or Celine right now. All I want is for you to heal.”

Johannes smiled weakly at Shana.

“What about Dalmar?”

“He’s dead,” Bari said. “He and his renegades were killed by UN peacekeeping troops after they tried to occupy another small town on the southern border. Dalmar and his troops all ended up getting blown to pieces, when they ran over one of their own IUD’s.” Bari said triumphantly. “By the way, you should know Shana saved your life.”

Johannes gave Bari a startled look. “What?”

“If Shana hadn’t called us from a cab, we would have never known where you were.”

Chapter 20

Six weeks had passed since Johannes was released from the Black Lion Hospital. He took Shana to meet his father. He once again gripped his father's brass doorknob with tight fingers as he'd done on many occasions. But today he wasn't afraid of his father's worsening health. He was concerned about how his father would react toward meeting Shana. He opened the door to greet his father.

Johannes' father smiled as usual when he saw his son enter the room. He sat up in his bed when he saw Shana standing next to Johannes, holding his hand. He motioned for Johannes and Shana to come in. He looked up at Johannes and spoke softly. "Yasmeen was right. She told me your fiancé was beautiful."

Johannes smiled at his father's compliment. He pulled a tissue from the box to wipe the tears falling from his father's eyes.

"Come closer, my dear," he said to Shana. "Let me look at you." Prince Dula took Shana's hand and said, "Thank you for saving my son's life." Tears of joy rolled down his cheeks. "I am happy my son has finally found a woman he loves enough to marry. You both have my blessing."

Johannes was surprised at his father's

enthusiastic acceptance of Shana. "Father, her name is Shana Zachary."

"Such a beautiful name."

Shana sat in Johannes' chair by his father's bed and smiled. Prince Dula strained himself but found enough strength to lift Shana's hand to his lips. "Welcome to my family." He said kissing her hand. "Now, I can rest assured my family's name will live on."

Johannes held his father's hand and smiled.

***

Shana and Johannes sat outside on the verandah watching the sky turn into a soft pink blush. As they watched the sun sink into the horizon, Johannes noticed Shana seemed quiet. He took her hand off the wrought iron chair. Stroking her hand softly, he said, "Shana, you are quiet tonight. Is anything bothering you?"

Shana looked up into the sky, brushing a gnat away from her arm. She didn't want to tell Johannes that after living in Africa, she had become a little homesick. Almost a year had passed since Shana had seen Lauren, her aunt, and Mr. Withers. She silently wondered how she would deal with these feelings on a long-term basis after they were married. "I'm fine, I was wondering...."

Johannes reached over and kissed her hand,

"Wondering about what, My Dove?"

"I was wondering what I'm going to do about a maid of honor for our wedding. I promised Lauren she could be my maid of honor if I ever got married."

Johannes hid his expression well. He didn't have the heart to tell Shana Lauren, her Aunt Helen and Mr. Withers had already made plans to attend the wedding. He wanted to surprise Shana. He smiled innocently and spoke in a soft voice, "do not worry Shana, you will find one."

"But, we don't have much time before our wedding. Don't get me wrong because I like Imani, and your sisters, but I always wanted Lauren to be my maid of honor."

Johannes continued to kiss and caress her hand, all the while, keeping his secret.

***

A week before the wedding, Johannes asked Rebecca to drive to the airport to pick up Lauren. She arrived on Ethiopian Airways flight 2039 at three fifteen in the afternoon. Lauren was one of the last to disembark. Rebecca knew her on site thanks to Johannes' description and her many discussions with Lauren. Rebecca waved to Lauren.

As Lauren declined the airplane steel stairs, Rebecca looked behind her and saw a man following her. When they both reached the ground, Rebecca smiled and promptly greeted them both. Lauren shook Rebecca's hand and introduced her friend. The man held out his hand and greeted Rebecca with a thick Spanish accent. Lauren introduced him as her boyfriend. "Rebecca, this is my fiancé, Carlos Latorre.

On the ride to the estate, Rebecca told Lauren about the bridal shower the wedding planner had planned for Shana later in the week.

Later in the afternoon Sifani and Stephanie arrived at the airport. The next day Shana's aunt arrived. All the guests were taken to the guest quarters adjacent to Johannes' estate where he had made arrangements for their lodging.

Finally, the day of the bridal shower came. Imani had previously told Shana she was giving her a bridal shower on Saturday. When Shana and Johannes walked into the gold reception room, the atmosphere was suspiciously quiet. Then out of nowhere music began playing. Guests came out from alcoves and hallways. Finally, Lauren came through the door holding walking between Shana's Aunt Helen and Senor Latorre. Tears flowed happily down Shana's face when she saw her family and friends. One of her sorority sisters from college whom she hadn't seen in ages followed her aunt and Lauren. She playfully punched Johannes in the arm and gave him a big kiss, then ran to greet Lauren and her Aunt Helen.

First she hugged her aunt and told her how much she had missed her.

“This isn’t a time for tears darlin,” her aunt stated as she patted her on the back. “You should be smiling from ear to ear now that you’re marrying this handsome prince.”

Shana laughed. Her aunt always made her laugh.

Then she looked at Lauren. “I have missed you,” Shana said, hugging her best friend.

Lauren’s eyes began to glisten. “Shana, I missed you too. My life is not the same at home since you’ve been gone.”

Then Senor Latorre came out of nowhere. Shana’s eyes lit up, “Senor Latorre! What on earth?”

Lauren walked over and kissed him on the lips. “Shana, I’ve been dying to tell you. Senor Latorre and I are engaged. But Johannes wanted to surprise you.”

Johannes had been standing back watching the entire show of affection, with great amusement.

Shana walked over to him. “Johannes, I don’t deserve you… I am truly blessed. Thank you.”

Johannes pulled her to his side and spoke

loudly, "We need to get on with the festivities." He took Shana by the arm and introduced her to everyone. Silence overcame the room when a nurse wheeled in his father.

His father waved his hand at everyone. Johannes and Shana walked over and gave him a big hug, and introduced him to her family and friends. "I think Prince Dula likes Shana's family and friends," Bari whispered to Stephanie.

After Prince Dula was wheeled away, Shana pulled Lauren and Senor Latorre to the side and gave them a curious look. "So when did all of this happen between you two?"

Senor Latorre spoke quickly speaking in a combination of Spanish and English, "Shana, the moment I met Lauren, I knew she would be my wife."

"I can't believe you," Shana replied. Then after a moment's pause she said, "You betrayed me, Lauren."

Lauren scrunched her nose and said, "Johannes made me keep everything a secret until your wedding." They all laughed.

After opening beautiful gifts, Bari raised his glass in a toast to his friends. "To two wonderful people that vast oceans and mighty continents could not keep apart, God Bless you!" Glasses clinked, and everyone applauded.

The day of the wedding, Lauren gasped when she saw Presidents and Prime Ministers from almost every country in attendance. Princess Sidha and her husband sat in the front row along with Johannes' father. Princess Yasmeen and Imani were two of Shana's bride's maids, and Lauren was her Maid of Honor.

Johannes stood tall, handsome and regal at the altar wearing his royal uniform, with Bari as his best man. Lauren, Princess Yasmeen, and Imani marched down the aisle wearing pale orchid chiffon gowns with beaded bodices and matching scarves draped around their necks. They all marched one by one down the aisle.

Finally, Shana walked down the aisle escorted by Mr. Withers' who gave her away. She wore a white organdy wedding gown and matching headdress made with yards of fabric. Her hair swept up in an elegant style. She looked more beautiful than ever. Though no one could see through the veil covering Shana's face. Gasps escaped the mouths of most of the guests as they admired how beautiful she looked when he lifted the veil. In a slow, deliberate pace, Johannes and Shana exchanged vows in English and Amharic.

"I love you," Johannes whispered to Shana.

"I love you back," she whispered in return.

"Are you sure you do not mind making Ethiopia your home?" Johannes asked.

“My home is where ever you are,” Shana replied.

Johannes beamed with pride. He lifted the veil, then placed his mother’s emerald ring on Shana’s left hand, third finger. “Wear this ring with pride because a famous woman once wore it.”

“Who?” Shana asked.

“The Queen of Sheba.” They both smiled and walked happily down the aisle.

THE END

Following is a list of books for further reading on the history of Ethiopia.

Brooks, Miguel F. Kebra Nagast (The Glory of Kings) Red Sea Press, 1998.

Davidson, Basil. Africa in History Macmillian Publishing Co., 1966.

Hansberry, William Leo. Pillars in Ethiopian History Howard University Press, 1981.

Jackson, John G. Introduction to African Civilizations Citidel Press, 1990.

Marcus, Harold G. A History of Ethiopia University of California Press, Reprint Edition, 1995.

Walker, Barbara G. The Woman's Encyclopedia of Myths and Secrets Harper Collins, 1983.

Beckworth, Carol and Fisher, Angela. African Ark: People and Ancient Cultures of Ethiopia and the Horn of Africa, Harry N. Abrams, Inc., Publisher, 1990.

Quick Order Form

Please send the following books. I understand that I may return any of them for a full refund—for any reason, no questions asked.

	QTY	PRICE	AMOUNT
KENTON'S VINTAGE AFFAIR	____	$10.00	$______
JUSTIN'S BODY OF WORK	____	$10.00	$______
CARTER'S HEART CONDITION	____	$10.00	$______
THE QUEEN OF SHEBA	____	$10.00	$______
Sales Tax & Postage			$______
Total			$______

(Please add $3.00 per book for California Sales Tax and Postage.)

Name:____

Address:______________________________________

City:______________________ State:____ Zip:_______

Email:____

My Check ____ Money Order____ is enclosed. Please allow up to six weeks for delivery.

To pay by credit card please email: kentepublications@gmail.com Our preferred method of payment is Paypal.com

Send completed form to:
KENTE PUBLICATIONS
P.O. Box 184
Jackson, CA 95642

Quick Order Form

Please send the following books. I understand that I may return any of them for a full refund—for any reason, no questions asked.

	QTY	PRICE	AMOUNT
KENTON'S VINTAGE AFFAIR	_____	$10.00	$______
JUSTIN'S BODY OF WORK	_____	$10.00	$______
CARTER'S HEART CONDITION	_____	$10.00	$______
THE QUEEN OF SHEBA	_____	$10.00	$______
Sales Tax & Postage			$______
Total			$______

(Please add $3.00 per book for California Sales Tax and Postage.)

Name:______________________________________

Address:____________________________________

City:____________________ State:____ Zip:______

Email:_______________________________

My Check ____ Money Order____ is enclosed. Please allow up to six weeks for delivery.

To pay by credit card please email: kentepublications@gmail.com Our preferred method of payment is Paypal.com

Send completed form to:
Kente Publications
P.O. Box 184
Jackson, CA 95642

www.ingramcontent.com/pod-product-compliance
Lightning Source LLC
Chambersburg PA
CBHW030917120626
46554CB00001B/178

* 9 7 8 0 9 6 4 3 3 4 9 7 7 *